SILENT NIGHT, DEADLY NIGHT

SUSPENSE SERIES - BOOK SIX

KAYLEA CROSS

SILENT NIGHT, DEADLY NIGHT

Copyright © 2020 Kaylea Cross

* * * * *

Cover Art & Print Formatting: Sweet 'N Spicy Designs
Developmental edits: Deborah Nemeth
Line Edits: Joan Nichols
Digital Formatting: LK Campbell

* * * * *

ISBN: 9798566487571

Dedication

For all my readers who love Christmas stories and the **Suspense Series** crew! Wishing you all a magical holiday season after an extremely tough year, and here's hoping 2021 will be much kinder to us all.

Kaylea

Author's Note

It's been a long time coming, but I'm thrilled to finally bring you a follow-up story for Luke Hutchinson and crew! You all know he's my favorite (but shhh, don't tell the other heroes—I don't want to hurt their feelings), so it was lovely to spend time with him and the others again. I hope you enjoy it.

Also, because of Christa you'll see a reference to women's softball being included in the Summer Olympics in this book. At the time I'm writing this, softball was to be included in the Olympic Summer Games held in Tokyo, July 2020. Due to the COVID-19 pandemic, the games have now been rescheduled for July 2021. I'm supposed to be attending the softball event there as a guest of Team Canada, so we'll have to see how everything shakes out over the next year.

Happy reading,
Kaylea

Chapter One

Emily Hutchinson grasped her husband's hand tightly as they stepped out of the clinic into the pleasantly cool December afternoon air. A blanket of cloud obscured the sun, and the breeze had the edge of a bite to it, not unusual for Christmastime in Charleston.

Neither of them said anything on the way to the parking lot, each of them caught up in their own heads, and right now hers was whirling like a tornado. Anxiety burned the pit of her stomach like battery acid, threatening to burn a hole through it.

Her doctor had called last week to say that her blood work had come back abnormal, and had scheduled all the follow-up tests for today. Now they were done, and all Emily could do was wait to find out what was happening.

Luke opened the SUV door for her, grim-faced and jaw tight, the gray light catching on the silver in his stubble. Even in his fifties he was still the most gorgeous man she'd ever seen.

She slid into the passenger seat without looking at him, afraid to in case it made her burst into tears, and ordered herself to get a grip on her fear. Luke was her rock and the strongest man she knew, but she was his weak point. She had to hold it together for his sake, put on a brave face through whatever came next.

She took a deep, slow breath while he went around to the driver's side, pushing down the bubble of panic rising inside her. *Calm down. You don't know what it means yet.*

But damn, she'd been doing so well. She'd been feeling so great, if a little tired and not having much of an appetite lately, though that was to be expected with everything she'd been doing to prepare for this week.

This cruel disease had taken so much from her already. Including her uterus and right breast. Tormenting her with all the side-effects from the chemo and radiation, the months of fear and uncertainty. The ever-present fear that it would come back.

Now it seemed it wanted even more.

You can't have any more of me, she told it, a hard seed of anger beginning to take root deep inside. *I won't let you.*

Luke slid into the driver's seat and closed his door, shutting the two of them in and the rest of the world out. She pretended to busy herself with finding something in her purse, not quite having herself together yet, then a big hand gently captured her jaw and turned her face toward him.

She swallowed, a spurt of anguish shooting through her as she stared into those intense, dark-chocolate eyes.

"We're going to face this and whatever else comes, together. Hear me?" His voice was low. Full of resolve. "One day at a time, sunshine. We take each day as it comes."

In other words, don't leap ahead and think of all the terrible things that could be coming down the road. Which she'd already done, the instant she'd gotten that initial call from the doctor, and kept circling back to every day since. How could she not? Having been a nurse almost made it worse. She knew the odds, and they weren't in her favor.

She nodded and forced a smile, ignoring the sting at the backs of her eyes. More than anything she wanted to burrow into him and hide in his protective arms. But even Luke, with all his strength and formidable skills, couldn't protect her from this.

Knowing what was coming made it so much worse, because she'd already been through it all before. The only blessing was at least this time she would have him by her side through whatever came next, and have him to lean on during the times when it all became too much.

"Yeah," she whispered, her voice slightly rough. "And just in case I don't say it enough, I really love you, you know."

Raw anguish flashed in his eyes for an instant before he masked it with his usual strong front. "I know. And I'll love you forever."

I know. She gave him another smile and gently pulled from his grasp, clearing her throat as she faced forward once again, determined to focus on something other than the fear that her cancer had returned.

Thankfully, she had something happy to look forward to right now. "We'd better get going, their flight just landed a few minutes ago."

Luke started the engine and drove out of the parking lot without another word. She punched a button on the dash to activate the radio, needing some kind of background noise to fill the silence. She had about twenty minutes to mentally shift gears before they reached the airport, northwest of the city.

Except... "Don't say anything to Rayne and Christa, okay? I want this to be a happy, stress-free visit for everyone, and I don't want them to worry. I've been looking forward to this for months."

He nodded once. "All right."

"Thank you." Dwelling on the future was pointless

3

at the moment, she told herself. They didn't even know what they were facing yet, and wouldn't until these new test results came back. It was also possible that everything would be fine.

But it's never been fine before, has it? that insidious little voice in her mind whispered.

She blocked it from long practice and instead concentrated on the upcoming reunion. Their son and daughter-in-law had flown down from Vancouver to spend the holidays with them, and the rest of their guests were due in tomorrow so they could all have an early Christmas celebration together—a mix of friends and Luke's colleagues who had become part of the family.

It was the first time they'd all been together since Rayne and Christa's wedding last November, and that harrowing time in Beirut when Luke had almost died saving her from the clutches of Tehrazzi early this year.

As terrifying as the ordeal had been, that fateful mission had changed her entire life for the better. Against all odds it had brought Luke back to her, and he'd never wavered in his support of love in the year since.

She no longer feared he would leave again. She trusted that he would stay with her through everything, to the end.

Thankfully, traffic was light and they made it to the airport in good time. Now that she'd made up her mind to put her health worries aside, excitement bubbled inside her, pushing away the lingering fear as she took Luke's hand and walked toward the terminal.

With all the people she loved best in the world about to be staying in their home, she had lots to occupy her mind and keep her busy. This was her favorite time of year. She wasn't going to let anything spoil it.

The arrivals terminal seemed busier than normal; no surprise given it was just a few days before Christmas. "Do you see them?"

"Not yet." Luke wrapped a solid arm around her shoulders and squeezed, and even though he didn't say anything else, she could hear his silent message. *I'm here for you. It's gonna be okay, Em.*

She hoped so. Either way, she was going to soak up every single moment of joy these next few days brought, and all the days she had left.

"There they are."

She pushed onto her tiptoes to see over the crowd flowing around them outside baggage claim, then gasped, her heart flooding. A giant smile spread across her face as she broke away from Luke, her feet already carrying her toward her son. "You're here!" she cried.

Rayne and Christa both looked up, their faces brightening. It still amazed her how much he looked like his father, except for his hazel eyes.

She rushed toward them, earning laughs as she flung herself into her son's waiting arms. Rayne caught her with a chuckle and hugged her tight. "Hey there, gorgeous."

Emily returned the embrace. Ohhh, she'd missed him. So much. They'd gone way too long between visits, almost seven months this time. "Hi. I'm so glad you're here." She pressed her face to his muscled shoulder and hugged him until her arms ached.

"Hey, save some of that for me," Christa said next to him in her adorable western-Canadian accent.

Emily let go of Rayne and reached for her daughter-in-law. "Don't worry, I've still got some juice left in these arms." She hugged Christa, her heart squeezing at the younger woman's genuine warmth. She'd fit into their family perfectly, and Emily couldn't imagine a better, more down-to-earth woman for her son. "I'm so glad you're here too."

"So am I. I can't wait to spend Christmas with you guys." Christa rubbed her back gently, then pulled away to smile at her, her aquamarine eyes sweeping over

Emily's face. "You look so great."

"Well, thank you." *But I'm still here*, that awful voice whispered out of nowhere. *Spreading inside you. You can't stop me.*

She ruthlessly shoved it away. She was done with being a victim, and had too much to live for. If this stupid disease wanted her, it would have to fight her to the bitter end.

She hooked an arm around Rayne's waist, leaning her head on his shoulder while Christa hugged Luke. Luke was still a little stiff about it, but getting better. It always amused her to see how awkward he was at hugging other people when he was so incredibly affectionate and comfortable with her.

"Y'all ready to get back to the house and have some good old Lowcountry cooking?" Emily asked. She'd made all Rayne's favorites, and things she knew Christa liked as well.

"She's been cooking for days," Luke said.

"*So* ready," Christa answered, allowing Luke to take her suitcase. She came to stand on Emily's other side and linked their arms. "Rayne's been wondering if you made him coconut cake. Because lord knows I've tried to make it enough times, but apparently it's not the same or as good as when you make it—even though I use the recipe you gave me." She shot her husband a censuring look.

Emily peered up at her son as he grinned at her and shrugged. "No one makes it like you," he said.

"Flatterer," she said with an easy smile. She adored him and they had a special bond she treasured.

"So, when's everyone else due in?" he asked as they neared the exit to the terminal.

"Two tonight, and the rest tomorrow," she answered, hardly able to believe the time was finally here. This was going to be such a wonderful few days, all of them together, safe and under one roof. "And I can't wait."

****

Lieutenant Declan McCabe hunkered down on one knee in the darkness of the desert night and used hand signals to direct his SEALs into position around the target building. It was oh-two-hundred hours, and the village was silent.

They'd taken out two sentries guarding the entrance at the main gate earlier, and so far, no one else had raised the alarm. No one knew they were here, but that was about to change.

Especially for the target hiding inside this house they had come to capture.

His men stacked up in formation beside the door they were about to infiltrate. The latest intel on their target had come from a reliable HUMINT source just hours ago, guaranteeing that the elusive Said Kader would be here. But the timeline was tight. Dec and his men had less than an hour to capture him and get him back to base.

After checking the perimeter one last time and making sure there were no booby traps, Dec gave the signal for the breach. The first man in line blew the lock on the door and kicked it in. The rest of the eight-man team poured through it, Dec going last while two more of his men stood guard outside. All other members of the platoon were positioned around the village to provide security and recon.

Faint ambient light coming through the barred windows of the house made his NVGs paint everything in bright green as they swept the rooms. "Clear," he whispered when they'd checked the lower floor and found it empty.

They started up the stairs. Dec went second to last, ready to fire at any moment. The final member stayed at the bottom of the steps to guard their six. Kader was the

CIA's current number one high value target. Deadly as they came, and trained by the same agency that now wanted him captured.

The first two bedrooms upstairs were empty. So was the bathroom.

Only the master bedroom at the end of the hall remained.

He locked his gaze on the door as his men approached it. When everyone was ready, he gave the signal. "Go."

They burst into the room. Fanned out to cover the corners.

There was no one there. Not a single person in the entire fucking house.

"Clear," he said, tamping down his irritation. Dammit. They'd been sure Kader was here. What the hell had happened?

He radioed HQ to give them his report. No joy. Premises empty, no sign of target.

"Roger that, Falcon Two. Return to base," the person on the other end said.

He turned to his men, hiding his frustration. They'd been hunting Kader for five weeks now. Twice before they'd executed ops to try and capture him. Now they'd come up short again, when they'd been closer to finding him than ever. Something wasn't adding up. They were being fed bad intel. "We're outta here, boys."

They went back out into the dark night air, joined up with the rest of the platoon and humped it the mile-and-a-half to the LZ to await their ride to base. The distant sound of the rotors reached them long before the silhouette of the approaching Chinook broke through the cloud deck.

Dec waited on one knee with his platoon while the massive helo landed, then directed them toward the tail ramp. The clock on this mission had run out. Their search for Kader was at a dead end.

But that wasn't his problem anymore. Because three hours from now, Dec and his guys would be wheels up for the long flight back Stateside.

Frustrated as he was about failing to nail Kader, he was very much looking forward to surprising his wife when he showed up at Luke Hutchinson's door in Charleston about twenty hours from now.

****

Joe stepped into the light and folded his arms, standing only a few feet from the prisoner strapped to the chair. The man had already undergone twenty-one hours of captivity and interrogation. He hadn't broken yet.

That was why Joe was here in person. He had too much riding on this to leave it to anyone else.

"Where is it?" he asked the prisoner softly, his breath misting in the cold air as the words were absorbed by the thick concrete walls. They were fifty feet below ground here in this abandoned, secret Cold War era facility where high value prisoners to the Agency had once been held.

There were no cameras or microphones down here. No one would interrupt them. No one else would hear the prisoner's screams.

Kader looked up at him through eyes so bruised they were almost swollen shut. Blood covered his face, his naked body covered with cuts and welts. He was trembling. Not from fear. From the cold.

"Where's what?" he slurred through battered lips, his words holding the faintest trace of an Arabic accent. Several of his teeth lay on the blood-spattered concrete floor.

Joe kept his expression impassive even as anger pulsed through him. "You know what. And I'm losing patience." He raised an eyebrow. "You know firsthand what happens when I run out."

A wheezy laugh answered, followed by a sharp

9

wince as it pulled on Kader's likely broken ribs. He drew in a shallow breath, his expression hardening, raw hatred in his expression. "I have n-nothing to s-say to you." His jaw shook, his body jerking with continual shivers.

Oh, you'd better.

Joe leaned his upper body toward him and dropped his voice to an ominous murmur. His sources on this were rock solid. "You talked shit about sending those files to someone. That you stole what belongs to me, hid them in a storage unit and planned to sell me out. But guess what? It's not happening. And you're gonna die either way." He was pretty sure Kader was bluffing about the files—but couldn't be sure.

Those swollen eyes focused on him, the defiance on that beaten face admirable, if futile.

Joe smiled. A slow, savage smile as he let the anger flow, and straightened. "Now. If you want me to make this as quick and painless as possible for you, you'll tell me where the storage unit is, and who you supposedly sent the intel to." The asshole thought it was his insurance policy. That he could blackmail Joe with it and save his neck. But he was wrong.

"If I don't check in with my c-contact within the next six hours, those f-files and the storage unit location will be sent to all the national n-news networks, and the Director." He paused, pulling in a shallow breath.

"You think that's gonna save you?" Joe said with an incredulous laugh. Threatening him with exposure to the Director of the CIA?

That stare never wavered. "You can k-kill me, but I'm t-taking you down with me."

He chuckled softly, the rage growing hotter. How dare he? How dare this piece of shit threaten him with this? "Not gonna happen." If this asshole really had sent the location and other incriminating evidence to someone, it would spell the end of Joe's and his accomplices' long and devoted careers serving their country. It might even mean their deaths.

Fuck that. Joe had spent over twenty years serving his country, doing the shitty, gray-area jobs no one else had the stomach for. He and the others deserved more than a government paycheck and a lousy pension plan for their service. He wasn't going down because of the wanted terrorist sitting in front of him.

Even as he thought it, a thread of alarm spiraled up his backbone. Along with a gut-deep certainty that this interrogation was going nowhere.

This asshole could have sent someone the evidence and storage unit location. Even after all the beatings, sleep deprivation and psychological torment, Kader still wasn't talking. He knew he was already dead, and yet refused to talk.

Torturing him further wouldn't do any good. Kader had no family or close friends left to threaten him with. And he was too well-trained to break.

Because Joe was the best trainer in the biz.

In a single motion he drew the pistol from the holster at the small of his back and put a bullet through Kader's forehead, the shot ear-splitting in the enclosed space. The body slumped over in the chair, held in place by the bindings as blood poured into Kader's lap and spilled onto the floor.

Joe holstered the weapon and turned, speaking to two of his men on the way to the door. "Get rid of the body. Then find out if he actually sent anything."

Two hours later he got the grim news from one of his associates. CCTV footage of Kader putting a small envelope in a mailbox just down the street from the motel he'd been captured at yesterday afternoon. Which meant that whatever the envelope contained was now well on its way to the recipient.

Joe clenched his jaw and lowered his voice as he

spoke into his phone. "Go back and tear apart every piece of evidence collected from his room. Find out who he sent that letter to, or we can all kiss our asses goodbye."

Chapter Two

Samarra Sinclair left the laundry room with a stack of folded clothes in her arms and hurried to the master bedroom, only to stop short in the doorway with a gasp of dismay at the sight before her. "What are you doing?"

Her husband Ben glanced up from where he was busy putting things—at the very last moment—into the carefully packed and organized suitcase she'd left open on the bed.

"Packing," he said, as though it was self-explanatory. "Don't worry, I'm Ranger rolling everything." He held up a folded shirt, winked at her, and made a show of rolling it tight before tucking it in between some of her carefully rolled-up clothing.

Her fingers clenched around the clothes she was holding, itching to shove him away and do it herself. "You're not taking your own suitcase?"

"Nah, I'm packing light, so it'll all fit in here just fine."

Sam stood there for another few moments, watching him, torn between annoyance and distress as he continued shoving his things in amongst hers. They'd married four months ago, in a double ceremony with his twin, Rhys, and wife Neveah. There hadn't been a dull moment since, with her and Ben just finishing up different contract jobs for the CIA.

Some things never changed, however. She was still the serious one and he loved to tease and pull pranks. While Ben still didn't fully understand her obsessive need for organization and tidiness, at least he didn't tease her about it like he used to.

After tucking his last shirt away, he straightened and glanced over at her. "You done with this?" He indicated the suitcase.

"Yes." She winced as he dumped one side of it on top of the other and began zipping it shut. Her OCD was going wild. All those things he'd shoved in there, mixed haphazardly with her own. There would definitely be wrinkles.

"You're so cute," he said with a grin, coming over to plant a big kiss on her lips.

"And you're lucky I love you so much."

"I know." He kissed her again, one hand slipping down to squeeze her ass.

She laughed lightly and pushed him away. "Don't get any ideas. We're on a tight schedule here."

"I always have ideas around you," he murmured, nuzzling the side of her neck.

If she hadn't been anxious about leaving on time, she would have enjoyed his attentions a lot more. "Stop distracting me. I have things to get done."

He swatted her butt. "Get to 'em, then. Slacker."

Somehow she resisted the urge to snatch the suitcase from his hands, rip it open and repack everything herself. Instead she made herself go into their walk-in closet and began putting everything away, either rolled-up neatly on the correct shelf, or hanging on hangers. The way civilized people put away their clothes.

She eyed Ben's side of the closet, suppressing a shudder. Absolutely nothing was organized by color. There wasn't a single label on the edge of any of the shelves, either. Chaos.

"Did you check for mail today?" she asked as she put away the last of her things. She'd already cleaned their place this morning while Ben was at the gym. It felt good to know that when they got home from this trip, they would walk into a tidy and clean house.

"No."

"I'll do it. How much longer are you gonna be?"

"Five minutes."

"'Kay." She strode down the hallway and grabbed the mail key from the dish on the table next to the door, telling herself to chill out more. He wasn't nearly as uptight as her when it came to schedules and things like that. But when flying she preferred to be at the gate early instead of barely clearing security as their flight boarded.

The front foyer was empty when she arrived in the lobby, unlocked their mailbox and grabbed everything inside. A lot of junk mail, a few bills, and...

She frowned at the plain white legal envelope. There was something small and hard inside it. It was addressed to her, but there was no return name or address, only D.C. marked on the stamp from the post office it was processed at.

She opened it on the way back to the elevator. A single, plain white sheet of paper was inside, with a flash drive and small metal key taped to it.

Someone had scrawled down a series of numbers on the page. Four in the top row, then two rows of seven beneath it. No explanation. No name or signature. Just the drive and key, and they had nothing written on them either.

Once back on her floor she hurried to the apartment. "Ben? You ready yet?"

"Two minutes," he called from the bedroom.

That should give her enough time to find out what was on this thing, and now she had something to focus on other than being anxious about him taking so long to get ready. She headed straight into her office, fired up her desktop, and plugged in the thumb drive, curious to find out what was on it. Seconds later, a screen of code popped up.

"What the hell is this?" she murmured, frowning. It wasn't like any code she was familiar with. Had to be encrypted. She could probably crack it with some software she had, but not now—they needed to leave for the airport. She'd take it all with her.

Unplugging the flash drive, she put it and the letter in her purse and checked her watch. Damn. "We're gonna miss the plane if you don't hurry." Yeah, he was a lot more relaxed than her, but there was such a thing as being *too* laid back sometimes.

"We're not gonna miss the plane." He appeared in the doorway, handsome as ever, his pale green eyes twinkling with amusement and his wide shoulders all but filling the doorframe. "I'm hungry. Wanna stop for a bite to eat on the way?" he teased.

"No." She marched past him out into the hallway, grabbing her carryon with her laptop in it. "So someone just mailed me a letter with only some numbers written on it, along with an encrypted thumb drive and a small key, and I don't have a clue who it was." She pulled her jacket from the hook by the door. "Or what it means."

The wheels of their suitcase clicked across the hardwood floor as he steered it to the door. "Did you open the drive?"

"Yeah. It's full of code I'll need to decrypt. So weird. The only thing I have to go on is that it was mailed from somewhere in D.C."

"Can I see it?"

"Sure, once we're at the airport." She gave him a sweet smile.

He grinned, cupped the back of her head with one hand and bent to kiss her. "Love you."

"Love you too, now hurry." She pushed him toward the door.

On the way to the airport she plugged the thumb drive into her laptop to get a better sense of what she was dealing with. The first two encryption programs she ran didn't work on it, and they were programs she used regularly for her contract work with the CIA.

"Crack it yet?" Ben asked as he merged them onto the freeway.

"No. The security on this thing is a helluva lot more advanced than the stuff I normally work with." That in itself raised red flags. Who was this from? Someone she knew? Why all the secrecy? "Gotta say, I'm not feeling so good about whoever sent this knowing my name and home address."

"You bringing it with you?"

"Of course. I need to find out what it is, and who it's from, so I know what I'm dealing with."

They made it to the pay parking in ample time to catch the next shuttle to the terminal. The whole time they went through check-in and security, she was thinking about the files and encryption. Whoever had sent it had access to fairly advanced technology, so she had to assume it was someone in the security or intelligence field. All the unanswered questions were driving her nuts.

As soon as she and Ben were through into the departures area, they found a secluded work area in the airline's private lounge. Making sure no one was around to see, Sam angled her laptop screen down to avoid any cameras picking up anything, then plugged the thumb drive back in without connecting to the Wi-Fi.

"Here's the note," she told him, handing over the

piece of paper.

Ben pulled up a chair beside her, the scent of the cin-namon-flavored gum he always chewed comforting and familiar. She was the one with the fancy degrees from MIT, but he was damn good with technology too, in addi-tion to being a former Ranger with a fifth-degree black belt.

He made her feel safe and she loved him to pieces—even though his off-kilter sense of humor and prankster tendencies sometimes drove her nuts. Opposites really did attract.

He studied it a moment. "Last two might be coordi-nates, but no clue what the first one means. Something to do with the key, maybe?"

"Maybe. I'm more interested in what's on this drive, to be honest." She quietly explained the previous pro-grams she'd tried, then activated a third.

Nothing. Same with a fourth and fifth. And she was running out of time to crack this before they had to board.

She blew out a breath. She loved solving mysteries and cracking codes, but not when they were potentially dangerous and mailed to her home. "Only got one more trick up my sleeve, then I've gotta reach out for help. And I'd rather not do that until I find out what this is and who sent it, just in case," she murmured, loading the final pro-gram.

Seconds after she started it, things began popping up on screen. Numbers. A list of them, in three columns.

"Those look like...bank accounts, and either depos-its or withdrawals." Ben leaned closer.

"Yeah, they do." Except the figures made absolutely no sense to her whatsoever. There were no names, no other information given. "Wonder what this is about?" It was all so strange. And unsettling. Someone had singled her out for this personally. Why?

"What about those other attachments at the bottom?"

Ben pointed to the three icons.

She entered some more code manually. One by one, the attachments began to unlock. Three images, showing the same man in various settings. Caucasian. Early to mid-forties, fit, with sandy-brown hair.

In one he wore military fatigues holding a weapon. In another he wore street clothes drinking a beer at some bar. The third was of him in profile, wearing business casual in some kind of meeting with other men.

"Recognize him? Because I don't," she said.

"No. Can you run facial diagnostics?"

"Not here." Not nearly enough privacy, and she'd need a secure Internet connection. Luke would have one.

She shook her head in frustration and examined the evidence before her. "Who the hell are you, and why did you send this to me?"

It creeped her out. She didn't like the feel of this at all. Why go to the trouble of sending this to her if there was no information about who this man was, or what this all meant? What did the sender want from her?

A female voice came over the speaker, announcing their flight to Charleston was boarding.

Sam quickly removed the thumb drive and shut down her laptop. This mystery would have to wait a while longer. "Let's get going. We'll have to do more digging once we get to Luke's place."

****

While Rayne was happy to be back home in Charleston for the holidays, he couldn't shake the nagging sense that something might be wrong. His mom had been ecstatic to see them at the airport, looking as elegant and put-together as ever, but something kept bothering him nonetheless.

She'd recovered beautifully since the end of her

cancer treatment, and for that he was grateful. He just hoped that having everyone here this week wouldn't be too much for her. She had a tendency to work too hard when she was in hostess mode, so he planned to watch her carefully and intervene if she overdid it. Which she inevitably would.

He jogged down the curving wooden staircase to the main floor of his parents' house, smothering a yawn. The stately brick house looked the same inside as it always had, cozy and immaculate, though it was still weird to know his dad lived here too now, after being absent from their lives for so many years.

He and Rayne had officially buried the hatchet before the wedding last fall, though things were still a little strained between them at times. He'd forgiven his dad for taking off on them when Rayne was a kid, but he hadn't forgotten.

Going forward, as long as his dad stuck around this time and made his mom happy, then Rayne was willing to let the past go. As messed up as his parents' relationship and family situation had been, they'd never stopped loving one another.

Mentally shelving all of that, he inhaled deeply, the familiar scent of lemon oil soap his mom used on the wood floors and furniture mixing with the mouthwatering aromas coming from the kitchen. His empty stomach let out an impatient growl.

He found his mom and Christa in the bright, cozy kitchen at the granite-topped island, making something together. "Please tell me that's coconut cake I smell baking."

They both looked up at him with smiles, and the sight of them working so comfortably together filled him with warmth. He was so lucky that they adored each other. "No, sorry, that's for tomorrow," his mom said. "It's chocolate stout cake."

"I like chocolate stout cake too."

"Don't I know it," she said with a wry smile.

He walked over to them, slung an arm around each and gave them a big squeeze, his heart full. Christa loved puttering in the kitchen as much as his mother did. "My two best girls."

He was an unapologetic mama's boy, and proud of it. His mom was the best, and as it had just been the two of them for most of Rayne's childhood and teen years, they'd always been incredibly close. As a result, he was naturally protective of her.

Christa and his mom exchanged grins, hugged him in return, then shooed him away. "Go make yourself useful and get us something to drink while we finish up," his mom said. "We're eating out on the back verandah. Your father put a heater out there for us."

"On it." He poured wine for the ladies, and got a beer each for him and his dad. The man himself walked out of the French doors onto the verandah a moment later carrying two platters laden with food. "Is that shrimp and grits?" Rayne asked eagerly. And homemade collard greens.

One side of his dad's mouth curved upward. "Yeah. She went all out for you guys." He set the platters down in the middle of the beautifully set table.

Ohhhh, *yum.*

Rayne handed his dad a beer and took one of the chairs opposite him, dying for the moment he could dig in. He and Christa had been up since four Vancouver time, and had only grabbed a sandwich during their layover in Chicago hours before.

He leaned forward in his chair and held out his beer toward his dad, a peace offering and homecoming all in one. He and his dad had their issues, but Rayne respected him a lot. Especially for a particular incident that had changed Rayne's life when he was eighteen.

While out drinking with friends one summer night, he'd wrecked his mom's car. He'd woken up the next morning, feeling guilty and hung over, to find his father standing at the foot of his bed. One look at his old man's face, and Rayne knew he was in the deepest shit possible. Having been notably absent for most of his formative and teen years, his father had dropped everything and flown in from Louisiana to drag Rayne's sorry ass off to the Marine Corps Recruit Depot in Parris Island.

Without a doubt, becoming a Marine had turned Rayne's life around, and if he was honest, he'd always secretly hero-worshipped his old man. Luke Hutchinson was a former SEAL legend and a genuine badass, and was no doubt climbing the walls of this house since he'd transitioned out of the field and into consulting work for the CIA months ago.

"Cheers," Rayne said to him.

His dad touched his bottle to Rayne's, his gaze warm. "Cheers."

Yeah, they'd come a long way in the past few years.

They both stood when the ladies came out a minute later carrying more food. Rayne groaned and snatched the platter of his mom's famous buttermilk biscuits from her. "It's enough to bring a tear to my eye."

She laughed and Christa snorted, rolling her gorgeous aquamarine eyes at him. "Yeah, because you're so hard done by in the food department at home," she said dryly.

"I know, I'm spoiled," he told her, looping an arm around her waist and kissing the top of her head. "But there's just nothing like your own mama's cooking."

Christa shot him a playful, narrow-eyed look. "You're lucky I still love you after that comment."

"He's *so* spoiled," his mom said with a fond smile.

"I am," he admitted. "But I spoil her too. Just not in the kitchen. Right, darlin'?"

Christa's cheeks flushed as she cleared her throat and immediately changed the subject. "Thanks for making all of this, Emily. It looks and smells amazing."

"It was my pleasure. Now." She raised her wineglass, smiling at them, and then his dad.

And it was only then under the light from the lantern hanging above them on the porch roof that Rayne noticed the proof of what his gut had already been telling him. Dark smudges beneath her eyes that she'd tried to conceal with carefully applied makeup.

His gut constricted instantly, dread snaking up his spine. She seemed a little thinner than the last time he'd seen her as well. Was she just tired, maybe stressed with all the prep for this week? Or...

She couldn't be sick again. Just couldn't.

"To family," she said, the joy on her face making his stomach hurt. He loved her so much. Couldn't bear the thought of her suffering any more. "Love y'all."

"Love you back," they all said, and Rayne held back the questions racing through his mind.

His mom looked so happy, even in spite of her fatigue. He didn't want to upset her by asking if she was okay, and there was a chance he was wrong. She might just be tired after getting everything ready for the holidays. She'd always gone all out at Christmastime.

"So, Christa, how's the training going?" his dad asked her, passing the platter of shrimp and grits across the table.

"Great, thanks. I'm in the gym five times a week with the national team trainer, and working out with the pitching staff three times a week as well. In the New Year we'll start team workouts and indoor practices until the weather warms up enough for us to go outside."

"Good lord, when do you fit in everything else, like your landscaping business?" his mom asked.

Christa smiled. "I manage. And it helps to have a

really great support network behind me." She nudged Rayne affectionately. "This'll be the first time softball has been back in the Olympics for a long while. I can't believe it's coming up so fast."

"Remind me where is it this time?" Emily asked.

"Tokyo, at the end of July. I'm so excited. Been working toward this for years and years."

"You deserve it." His mother turned to him. "Are you going?"

"Yeah, of course I am." He took the platter from Christa and served himself a big portion. He'd planned to wait until Christmas morning to give them their present, but now seemed like the perfect time. "And Merry Christmas, because we managed to get tickets for you guys as well. Opening ceremonies and the softball."

His mother's face lit up. "Oh, we'd love that! Wouldn't we, Luke?" she glanced at him, beaming.

"Wouldn't miss it for the world, darlin'," he said, giving Christa a wink. "We're damn proud of you and everything you've accomplished."

She blushed and murmured a thank you, but Rayne could tell the compliment thrilled her. Her own mom was the farthest thing from maternal and they didn't have much of a relationship, though her stepdad was pretty awesome. Rayne could see his parents' support meant the world to her.

"Not as proud as I am." He reached for her hand and squeezed it, still in awe of her.

He'd seen firsthand how hard Christa had worked to make the national team. All the sacrifices she'd made, balancing training with her landscaping business to pour her heart and soul into the sport she loved to achieve her dream. He couldn't wait to watch her walk into the stadium at the opening ceremonies wearing a Canadian maple leaf with her teammates.

"Thanks, babe." She smiled at him as she passed him

the collard greens.

He spooned a healthy portion onto his plate, his mouth watering. "So, when does everyone else get in?"

His mom put a freshly baked biscuit onto his and Christa's plates. "Ben and Sam should be here in an hour or two. Rhys and Neveah get in tomorrow at lunchtime, and Bryn sometime tomorrow night."

He and Bryn had been friends for over fifteen years now, ever since meeting the first time he'd gone down to a family friend's beach house in Lincoln City, Oregon. He'd gone back at least once every year since, but he and Bryn stayed in touch in between visits. Now she and Christa talked all the time too.

"What about Dec?" he asked. Bryn's husband, an active duty SEAL.

"He's OCONUS," his dad answered. "Not sure if he'll be able to make it."

"But he's going to try," his mom said.

The meal was everything Rayne could have hoped for, and then some. The conversation flowed easily around the table while they ate, and his parents asked him about his work on an RCMP Emergency Response Team in Vancouver. Every bite brought a childhood memory, and being able to share it with his whole family made it all the more special. If he could have shaken the worry about his mom, it would have been perfect.

After he and his dad cleaned up the dishes, he left Christa chatting with his mom in the living room with some tea by the fire and headed for the study. He knocked, received a brusque reply to enter, and slid the pocket door open.

His dad was seated behind the antique mahogany desk, busy on his computer. He looked up at Rayne, and when Rayne didn't say anything, raised his eyebrows. "Something on your mind?"

Rayne shut the pocket door and leaned against it,

KAYLEA CROSS

unable to shake the dread. "Anything you wanna tell me?"

"About what?"

"About Mom."

Just like that his dad's expression shuttered, and Rayne's stomach dropped. "She's fine."

Christ, so she *was* sick. "She doesn't look fine, she looks exhausted. And don't bullshit me. If something's going on, I want to know."

His dad sighed and leaned back in his chair to study him. "She's worried. We don't know what's happening exactly, we're still waiting on more test results she had today. And don't you dare say anything, because I promised I wouldn't tell you, and I don't want her getting upset."

"I won't." One thing he couldn't fault his father for was how protective he was of his wife. Rayne ran a hand over his face, reeling inside. "How serious is it?"

"We're not sure yet."

Jesus. The delicious meal he'd just enjoyed was now sitting in the bottom of his stomach like a ball of concrete. "Is there anything I can do?"

"Just let her enjoy every moment of having you and Christa here. You know you're her world."

Rayne nodded, wishing he could actually *do* something to make it better. A rush of sadness shot through him, sharp and acidic. His mom had been to hell and back more than once already, and had suffered far too much pain in her life.

It wasn't fair. He couldn't accept that the cancer was back, afraid that she wouldn't be able to beat it this time.

The sound of the doorbell made him and his dad look at each other. "That'll be Ben and Sam," his dad said, rising as Rayne straightened.

Rayne let his father pass and stayed in the study for a few moments to collect himself. More than sad, he was getting angry now. *Fuck you, cancer.*

He drew a deep, steadying breath. Whatever happened, if this was going to wind up being their last Christmas together, then Rayne wanted it to be a holiday none of them would ever forget.

Chapter Three

"So how's civilian life treating you?" Ben asked him.

Luke reached into the fridge to grab him a cold beer. "As well as can be expected." At least he got to be home with Em.

Ben grinned. "You're bored to shit, aren't you?"

He let out a low laugh. "Sometimes." After doing what he'd done his entire adult life, suddenly being out of the action was a jarring—and not always easy—transition. "They keep me busy with various things that come up." But it wasn't the same. "I don't travel much anymore, at least not overseas very often."

"And you're finally going gray on us, I see."

Luke lifted an eyebrow at him. He'd just turned fifty-two. "Yeah. And I've earned every single one of them."

"True enough." Ben grinned and saluted him with the bottle.

"He's turning into a silver fox," Sam said with a wink, and carried her mug of tea through to the living room to join the others.

Luke followed with Ben, and found Em in her element, her daintily slippered feet curled up under her on the sofa as she talked with the others while a fire crackled in the grate next to her. The glow of the flames flickered over her face, blending with the white lights on the Christmas tree in the corner.

She laughed at something Rayne said, and Luke couldn't help but stare. She was so damn beautiful, inside and out, and this was the first time in weeks he'd seen her this happy and relaxed. She deserved every bit of happiness she could find.

The thought of anything taking her away from him now, after all they'd been through, after all they'd withstood, was unthinkable.

He shoved it from his mind before it could take hold, refusing to give it screen time in his head. Tough as the health scare was for them, having a house full of guests right now was actually a blessing.

Em had been born and raised in Charleston, and was every inch the Southern lady. She loved to entertain, loved taking care of those closest to her, and spending the next few days with their extended family would help keep her mind off everything. She'd known Bryn for years through Rayne, but the others she'd only gotten to know over the past year because they all worked with Luke.

Em had become especially close to Nev since then. It had started because of Em's health and Nev being a doctor back during the mission in Beirut earlier this year, but now they talked all the time and Em considered her part of the family. And also, by extension, Nev's taciturn husband, Rhys.

Now there was an interesting dynamic. Rhys was the polar opposite of his outgoing, prankster twin. He might seem antisocial to most, but Rhys was one of the best operators Luke had ever worked with, and Luke considered him a good friend.

Having Nev here to help keep an expert eye on Em's health over the next week would take a load off Luke's mind. Whatever happened, he didn't want his wife stressing about the status of those tests, though he knew she was still worried.

All in all, he'd never been so glad to be "retired." Whatever happened going forward, he would be at her side, and being home with her helped take the edge off craving the action of being out in the field.

She glanced up when he entered, her little smile hitting him square in the heart. God, he loved her. Her warmth and kindness, her unbelievable bravery through everything she'd faced, and the steely core inside the comparatively fragile-looking exterior. His Em was a fighter, and he'd be right there to fight beside her every step of the way through this.

He'd done a lot of unforgiveable things in his life, mostly in the line of duty—with one glaring and spectacular exception. It didn't matter that she'd forgiven him for accidentally putting that scar beneath the edge of her jaw and then taking off on her and Rayne all those years ago. For essentially abandoning her, and leaving her to raise their son and then later fight the battle for her life alone.

He still hadn't—couldn't—fully forgive himself for hurting her and walking out on them. But he'd thought of them every day they were apart. He'd never stopped loving her, not ever, and now that she was miraculously his again, he made it his mission to be the husband she deserved every day.

She shifted on the sofa and patted the cushion next to her. Luke sat down and stretched an arm across her shoulders, his chest tightening at the way she curled into him, the light, familiar scent of her vanilla perfume scenting the air. Her trust and unwavering belief in him never failed to humble him.

"Rayne was just telling a funny story about helping Christa at a national team practice a few weeks ago," she said as Ben and Sam sat together near Rayne and Christa.

"Only a few players could make it because the coach called an extra workout at the last minute, so I thought I'd give them a hand at the indoor field." Rayne shook his head, looking down into his wife's face with a sardonic expression. "They put me at third to do some pick-off plays. The next pitch came in and Christa fired the ball at me from behind home plate. I wasn't ready for it. Barely got my glove up in time to stop it from taking my head off."

Christa laughed. "I wasn't worried. I knew your reflexes would kick in."

"Glad you're keeping him on his toes," Luke said with a grin. He was happy to see that Christa had come out of her shell since first meeting him. She'd been so quiet and shy that first time at his old place in Louisiana. Now she was comfortable being herself around them.

"We should have a slo-pitch game when everyone gets here," Ben said, and everyone looked at him. "What? It'd be fun."

Sam poked him in the ribs. "You just want an excuse to strut around in your BoSox gear in front of everyone."

He grinned. "Well, that too."

The conversation carried on easily around the room after that, inevitably shifting to the times they'd spent together over the last few years—a lot of tough times in dangerous circumstances now glossed over with gallows humor. Christa and Rayne didn't know the others as well as they knew Bryn or Dec, but they knew enough, and had heard the stories of working ops with Luke.

Family wasn't always something you were born into, and this proved it. They'd all shared blood, sweat and tears together, forging a bond that could never be broken.

After a while, Ben got up to take Luke's empty bottle while Em was talking to Christa. "Can we talk to you alone for a minute?" Ben murmured to him.

Luke met that pale green gaze, searching for any sign

of concern, but couldn't get a read on Ben's expression. "Sure." He leaned over to kiss Em on the top of the head. "Excuse me a minute, sweetheart." As soon as he got up, Sam did too. She and Ben followed him to the study.

Luke flipped on the light, waited for them to enter then shut the pocket door behind them, crossing his arms over his chest. If they'd brought him in here for a private update, it must be important. "Something wrong?"

Sam shared a look with Ben before replying. "We're not sure, to be honest." She pulled something from her pocket. A flash drive. "Someone sent this to me at our home address, along with a key and a note. It arrived this afternoon just before we left for the airport. I was able to crack the encryption on the electronic files, and we think the numbers on the note might be coordinates, but I need to keep analyzing the data. Can I work on it in here? I need a secure connection, and I'd rather have privacy and not have to answer questions from anyone while I work."

Luke already didn't like the feel of this. "Where was it sent from?"

"D.C.," Ben said. "It's a list of bank accounts, and some photos of a guy we don't know. Sam's gonna try some facial recognition programs to see if she can get a hit."

Luke turned his attention to her. "Why you?"

Sam shook her head. "I have no idea why anyone would want to send it to me. I'm in between contract jobs right now with the Agency, just finished my latest one a couple days ago. As far as I can tell, this isn't related."

Luke glanced between the two of them, weighing the possibilities in his mind, and not liking any of the conclusions he came to. His gut said this was significant. "Can you trace where the bank accounts are, and who they're registered to?"

"I plan to, as long as you don't mind me working on it from here. It's uh, not exactly legal."

He nodded. He was no stranger to living in the gray area of the law. That's how things got done in his world. "That's fine. Anything else?" It also bothered him that Sam had received all this on the day she'd flown down here.

Had someone used her because of her connection to him? Lord knew he still had plenty of enemies out there, even though he hadn't been out in the field since Beirut earlier this year. These days he stuck close to home as often as possible, and to Em. She was his number one priority.

"No. Just wanted to give you a heads up, and make sure you were okay with us digging from here. There's a chance that someone could be monitoring activity on this. I don't want to share what I've found with anyone at the Agency until I know what I'm dealing with."

"Understood." Once she did, he could contact Jamie, his former boss. He was the only one Luke trusted in the whole Agency. "Let me know if you find anything concrete. I've still got some contacts we could use without triggering the Agency's notice." People who owed him favors and would keep their mouths shut if he told them to.

Sam gave him a relieved smile. "That'd be great. Thanks."

Luke waved a hand at his desk, wanting answers. Sam was a hard, dedicated worker. When she sank her teeth into something, she didn't let go until she'd finished the job. "Make yourselves at home. If anyone asks what you're doing I'll just say you're finishing up some last-minute things to clear the deck for when the others get here."

"Perfect," Ben said, clapping him once on the shoulder.

Luke stepped out into the hall and closed the pocket door behind him, wondering about the contents of the flash drive and what the key was for. Sam was incredible at what she did. Luke was certain she'd find answers to their questions soon enough.

Rayne was just coming into the kitchen when Luke passed by moments later. His son set some empty beer bottles in the recycling bin under the sink and turned to face him. "Mom looks happy."

He nodded, struck again by the man Rayne had become. They had slightly different coloring, and Rayne was taller with a larger build, but there was no doubt he was Luke's son. Luke was damn proud of him. "She does. She's been looking forward to this for a long time."

"We'll have to make sure she doesn't wear herself out."

Luke half-smiled. Their son was protective as hell of Em, and Luke admired him for it. "I'm on it."

Rayne covered a yawn and shook his head. "I'm beat. Think we'll turn in soon."

"Sure." And speaking of that… It was already almost ten. Em had been up at six to get the house ready, even though he'd already helped her clean it from top to bottom and put fresh sheets on all the beds yesterday. She needed to rest.

He found her still talking with Christa in the living room. "Did Ben and Sam turn in?" she asked him.

"No, they're just finishing up some work they need to get done."

"Chris and I are gonna hit the hay," Rayne said, crossing over to envelop Em in a hug. "G'night. See you in the morning."

"Night, son." She squeezed him tight, her face all but glowing with happiness. As soon as Rayne and Christa left the room, she popped up and started tidying and fluffing cushions.

"You ready for bed?" he asked, following her into the kitchen with some plates a moment later.

She didn't look back at him as she started rinsing dishes in the sink, already back in busy-bee mode. "In a bit. I want to get a head start on—"

Luke stepped up behind her, then reached around her and turned off the faucet. Settling his hands on her hips, he turned her to face him, then boosted her up onto the kitchen counter, bringing their gazes level.

Her gorgeous green eyes blinked at him in surprise as he ran a hand up her slender back, the shadows under them worrying him. She needed all her strength to fight whatever was happening inside her body. He wasn't going to stand by and watch her exhaust herself this week.

"I'll finish up here. And whatever else needs to be done can wait until tomorrow," he said in a low voice.

"Yes, but—"

He cupped the back of her neck and silenced her with a kiss. She didn't protest, her hands settling on his shoulders as her lips softened under his.

Luke moved in closer, settling deeper between her open thighs. He took his time with the kiss, coaxing and seducing, banding an arm around her back as he eased his tongue into her mouth. Giving her time to empty her mind of all the things she thought she needed to do, and focus on the here and now with him.

Her fingers tightened on his shoulders, a little hum of pleasure coming from her throat as she arched into him. And just that fast, arousal punched through him, hot and intense.

He touched his tongue to hers, caressing, teasing, then retreated to kiss the corner of her mouth. Her jaw. The scar he'd left with the point of his knife. A mark he could never erase but would spend the rest of his life making up for.

"Come to bed, Em," he murmured against her skin.

She was the love of his life. How the hell he'd managed to get through the empty wasteland of his life without her for so many years, he didn't know, but he'd been frozen inside. Encased in ice until her touch and her love had once again magically melted it away.

He felt the shape of her smile form under his lips. "Okay," she whispered, and looped her arms around the back of his neck.

Luke shifted and scooped her up in his arms, heading for the stairs while desire pulsed through him. Em curled into his chest, her soft weight pressed against his torso as she nuzzled the side of his neck. She loved it when he took charge like this, and it worked for him every bit as much as it did for her. Getting her revved up and then getting her off was his favorite thing in the world.

Pushing their bedroom door open with his foot, he shut it behind them and carried her over to place her on their king-size bed. Em sat up and reached for his shirt, her mouth capturing his as her fingers hurriedly undid the buttons.

Luke shrugged it off, stripped off everything else and came down on top of her in the darkness, wedging his hips between her thighs and drinking in her soft, sensual moan. Without breaking the kiss, he leaned over and switched his bedside lamp onto the lowest setting.

She made a sound of protest and stopped in the act of pulling her shirt off, but he grasped the material and eased it over her head, silencing her protests with another kiss. "I want to see you," he whispered, hard and aching for her.

She was still self-conscious of her mastectomy scars, and he was determined to make her believe she was more beautiful to him than ever. "Want to see your face when I make you come." He kissed her again, slid his hand beneath her to unhook her prosthetic bra.

She let him. Didn't cringe or curl in on herself as he drew it away. Instead her eyes stayed locked with his, her arms coming around his back. "I love you," she murmured.

Luke groaned and captured her mouth again, sliding his palm across her surgical scar before finding and cupping her left breast, drinking in her little gasp of pleasure. He'd lost too many damn years with her as it was.

Each day they had together was precious and he was going to savor every single moment of whatever time they had left.

****

"Oh, wow..."

Ben pushed to his feet and came around the desk to stand behind Sam so he could see the screen of her laptop. The house was still and quiet, everyone else having gone upstairs a while ago. "What'd you find?"

"Facial recognition software just got a hit." She typed something, clicked on a file. "This guy is in all the photos." She looked up at him. "You recognize the name?"

Joseph Hanes. He frowned, thinking. "It's...familiar." But he couldn't place it off the top of his head.

"Well, according to my sources, he's an Agency paramilitary ops officer."

Just like Luke had been. "Think he's linked to the accounts?"

So far Ben had managed to trace over half of them to their banks of origin. All offshore in various countries, registered to several different companies. He'd bet his left nut they were all shell companies, used to funnel dirty money out of the U.S. What kind of dirty was anyone's guess.

"Wouldn't be surprised." She leaned back and rubbed her fingers over her eyes, then lowered her hands into her lap and peered up at him. "Think Luke might know him?"

"Good chance he would." Luke was a legend for a reason in the intel community. He knew everyone who was anyone in that world.

Sam raised her dark auburn eyebrows. "Think he's still up?"

"Maybe." He'd heard Luke and Emily go upstairs about an hour ago. Rather than go check upstairs and risk interrupting anything, Ben shot him a text. *You still awake?*

The response came back seconds later. *Find something?*

Affirm.

Be down in two minutes.

"He's on his way down. Can you pull up the shot of Hanes in the BDUs? It's taken on a base somewhere. I wanna see if we can find anything in the background that might—"

The laptop beeped, drawing their gazes to the screen. "Hold on. Program just found another possible match." She brought up the diagnostics. Ben studied them along with her. Eighty-five-percent probability of a match based on various data.

"It's this guy," Sam finally said, tapping on the image of a man standing in the background of the shot Ben had been asking about, just behind Hanes's shoulder. Light brown skin. Either tanned Caucasian or maybe light-skinned Middle Eastern descent, and wearing military BDUs.

Whoever this other guy was, he and Hanes clearly knew each other well. Well enough to work together?

The pocket door opened. Luke came in wearing the same jeans and shirt he'd had on earlier. Sam waved him over, bringing up the first match. "We got two matches from the photos, according to the software. Here's the first one."

Luke stepped over to them, looked at the screen, and

his face tightened. "Joe Hanes," he muttered.

Ben looked at him sharply. "You know him?"

Luke nodded once, gaze hard. "We've met."

Knowing Luke, that could mean any number of classified things, and it was clear Luke wasn't a fan of the guy. "What do you know about him?"

"Last I heard he was in Syria working an HVT."

"How long ago?"

"Couple weeks."

"And what about this guy?" Sam asked, bringing up the other photo.

"Shit," Luke muttered, straightening to set his hands on his hips.

Ben cranked his head around to stare at him, alarm bells going off in his head. He knew that tone, and it never meant anything good. "What?"

"That's Said Kader."

Whoa. Ben frowned as he looked back at the image on screen, trying to make sense of it. He'd heard about Kader, especially over the past few weeks. "He's a terror-ist."

"One of the Agency's top ten HVTs. Hanes was tasked with capturing or killing him," Luke added, his gaze shifting to Sam. "He sent this to you?"

"No idea," she murmured, bringing up more information while Ben and Luke read over her shoulder. Sure as shit, Kader's name appeared on all kinds of things on the Agency's radar.

Luke shook his head, still watching Sam. "Why you?"

"I have no idea. I don't even know him—or Hanes." Her brown eyes swung up to him. "But you do. So maybe whoever sent it knows my connection to you, and…"

Ben's insides tightened as her unfinished sentence hung in the air, her words confirming the fear stirring in his gut. Someone knew way too damn much about them, and had just landed them in the middle of a shit sandwich. Possibly to target Luke, anticipating that Sam would reach out to him.

"No. If that was the case, the sender would have sent it to me directly," Luke muttered.

Ben wanted to know more about this HVT, Hanes, and Hanes's connection to Luke, because the timing of this whole thing was fucking suspicious, and he didn't want Sam or anyone else in this house in harm's way ever again. "Can you confirm whether—"

"Yeah, I'll check with someone right now," Luke said, pulling out his phone.

Ben folded his arms and chewed harder on his gum, his mind racing—to all kinds of terrible conclusions. Sam was nibbling on her lower lip as she studied the data, a frown knitting her forehead.

He hated that she was at the center of whatever this was. It made him want to whisk her out of here and take her off grid to a secluded cabin somewhere until they got to the bottom of it and confirmed she wasn't at risk. He was paranoid and protective like that.

"Roger, it's Hutch," Luke said to whomever he'd called. "Sorry to call so late. Listen, I wonder if you can verify two assets' locations for me." He met Ben's gaze. "Joe Hanes, and Said Kader." He listened for a few moments, then nodded once. "All right, thanks. Appreciate it. Merry Christmas, brother."

"Well?" Ben prompted as Luke lowered the phone.

"Hanes is back Stateside, just had meetings in D.C. with some higher ups the other day. And Kader was reportedly KIA in a drone strike the day before that in Idlib. Courtesy of Hanes and crew."

The tension in Ben's stomach eased, the all-too familiar burn disappearing as relief washed through him. Kader was dead. No crazy terrorist was gunning for Sam, or Luke. Crisis averted. "So then...who sent Sam the letter?"

"No damn idea," Sam murmured, frowning at her screen.

Someone who had a score to settle against Hanes. "The accounts must mean something. We can dig into them more tomorrow, find out what the deposits and withdrawals mean, and go from there."

He laid a hand on her shoulder and squeezed gently, relieved she wasn't in danger from this. "And on that note, let's call it a night." If he didn't force her to stop now, his little workaholic would still be sitting in here with her laptop come morning.

"All right," Sam said, sounding disappointed as she started shutting everything down.

"Let me know when you find out who the companies behind those accounts are registered to," Luke said. "Sleep well, but not too late. Em'll be in the kitchen at daybreak fixing breakfast for everyone no matter what I say, and you'll hurt her feelings if you miss it."

Ben grinned, feeling at ease once more. "I love that woman." He squeezed Sam's shoulder, looking forward to getting her naked in their room so he could shut her brain down with more enjoyable things for a while. "Come on, sweets. There's a fancy, antique four-poster waiting for us upstairs with our name on it." And he planned on making the most of it with his gorgeous wife.

Chapter Four

"Give me good news," Joe said to his guys as he walked into the condo currently serving as his safehouse.

From the moment he'd seen the video footage of Kader putting that envelope into the mailbox, his team had been trying to find out who he'd sent it to, with no luck so far. They didn't know what the envelope contained, but Joe could guess.

A hard copy of electronic files Kader hoped to destroy him with. Maybe even a location for the storage unit. Joe couldn't be sure whether Kader had been bullshitting him about that, trying to save himself with lies and an empty threat.

Of course, that threat might also be real.

Joe pulled in a steadying breath, beyond agitated. He needed to know where that fucking storage unit was. Everything he needed to start over was in there, but it had to stay a secret. And knowing Kader, the bastard had likely left some other kind of evidence that would end Joe as well.

He shook his head in disgust, rage building deep inside him. For Kader to try to take him down after everything that asshole had done in Syria? Crimes that even Joe didn't have the stomach to pull off? Fuck that.

"I've been ripping apart files from the laptop we recovered in his motel room," Joe's tech whiz replied. "From what I can tell, everything points to one person. He'd been searching for her—"

"Her?"

"Yeah, and he tried to look up her home address in the Agency files too."

Joe was still stuck on the last part. Since when did Kader have female contacts here? Let alone within the Agency? "He sent it to a female Agency employee?"

"Best I can tell she's a contract employee, civilian. The name Samarra Sinclair mean anything to you?"

Joe stilled, something catching at the back of his mind. "It's familiar." Her first name, at least. But he couldn't remember why, other than it was the name of a city in Iraq. "Can you pull up a picture of her?"

Five seconds later, Joe was looking at a familiar face. Deep auburn hair, brown eyes, freckles. Recognition flickered to life. "Samarra Wallace," he murmured, stunned as he finally placed her. She must have gotten married or something, explaining the surname change.

The tech guy looked up at him. "So you know her?"

"I know *of* her. She worked with Luke Hutchinson on various ops a while back." Joe knew him, but not well. More like he was aware of Hutchinson's reputation. One of the best operatives in the Agency's history, and a man you didn't want to cross.

"Did you get her address?" And what was Kader's connection to her? Joe didn't see how they would know each other. Unless Kader had reached out to her on a hunch because of her connection to Hutchinson.

"Yep. About a fifteen-minute drive from where Kader dropped the envelope into the mail. I've already pulled up the building specs."

Perfect. "Can you disable the security from here?"

The guy gave Joe an insulted look. "Of course."

"Good. Then let's get moving."

He and two of his guys hopped in an SUV and drove to the condo building near Alexandria. Just before they arrived, his tech wizard informed them that Samarra and her husband had left the building yesterday afternoon and hadn't come back, according to the security surveillance footage.

Perfect.

Someone in the foyer let them in as they reached the door, then they took the stairs to the sixth floor. All of them were armed. As far as Joe knew, Samarra was a tech and security expert, but didn't have the kind of training he worried about. Still, they needed to take care of any security measures before entering.

They paused at the condo door, noting the position of the security cameras in the hallway. Joe texted his tech guy to verify that he had taken care of the cameras. Joe had other tools and gadgets with him to take care of any alarm system inside.

He picked the lock on the door while the others kept watch, quickly located the alarm keypad inside the entry, and set his specialized electronic gadget against it. Seconds later, a green light flashed on the keypad, signaling the code had been entered.

"We're in, but keep an eye out for other cameras," he told the others in a low voice.

The three of them spread out to search the condo. One of them worked with their tech guy to break into the desktop computer and clone it.

Joe still couldn't see how Kader knew Samarra. But since Hutchinson had personally selected Samarra to work with him on various ops, it meant she was damn good at what she did, because Hutchinson only worked with the best. Joe had to assume she was smart enough not to keep anything sensitive on her home computer, but it wouldn't hurt to check. He needed what Kader had sent her.

His guys found three hidden cameras that had already been disabled as he'd first bypassed the alarm on the way in. He didn't find any other electronics of use in the place. No keys that looked like they belonged to a storage locker, no notes with anything promising on them. But when he pulled open the cupboard beneath the sink, he found an empty white envelope in the recycling bin.

Bingo. "Got the envelope." Her name and address were scrawled on it in Kader's hand, and the postmark confirmed it had been sent from D.C.

Unfortunately, there wasn't anything else in the bin to help him find what he needed. "Any flash drives or keys? Letters?" he called out to the others.

"Negative." One of his guys came out of the office. "Just waiting for Tim to crack her password so we can take a look at what's on her computer."

Joe did another sweep of the condo on his own, searching under drawers and cabinets, and looking at the back of the closets and inside the heating vents. Nothing. Dammit.

He was just walking into the kitchen after completing his search, when his phone beeped with a text from Tim. Joe called him immediately. "You in?"

"Yeah. She downloaded some files onto her desktop yesterday afternoon and then erased them. From what I can tell, they were all encrypted. It'll take a while for me to crack them."

Fucking Kader. If he weren't already dead, Joe would hunt him down and make him suffer more for this. "He must have sent her a flash drive, maybe the storage locker location. There's nothing here, so if she has it, she must have taken everything with her."

And if she had received electronic files from Kader,

it was possible she might already have sent them to some-one else. Shit.

"Well, then that means whatever she has is currently in Charleston."

Joe stopped in the middle of the kitchen. "What?"

"I'm looking at her emails now," Tim continued. "There's one confirming her and Ben Sinclair flying to Charleston yesterday afternoon. Their flight left not long after she downloaded the files initially."

The wheels in his head spun. "Hutchinson lives in Charleston."

He'd heard that Hutchinson had reconciled with his wife there a while ago. And it seemed like way too much of a coincidence for Samarra to have received Kader's let-ter the same day she and her husband left for Charleston, when she was so closely connected to Hutchinson.

Was she heading down there to see Hutchinson? Had Kader sent her the letter knowing she would?

Joe's pulse picked up. He needed to do immediate damage control. "Track them. All three of them."

Christ, this was getting more and more complex with each piece they unraveled. If Samarra had received the kind of intel Joe assumed Kader would send, she'd prob-ably tell Hutchinson.

And then Joe would be in even deeper shit than he already was. Because with one phone call, one email, Hutchinson could destroy him.

Joe had to stop this now. It was probably already too late to stop the spread of any electronic files she may have been sent.

But he could still get to Samarra, and find out if she had the location of the storage unit. Stop her from leaking that, and using anything else Kader had sent.

"Get us on a flight down there ASAP," he told Tim, "and see if you can find a rental car listing for them."

Joe would have to somehow get Samarra away from

her husband—and maybe Hutchinson as well if she was planning on paying him a visit. Taking her without much time to prep, and possibly while she was under Hutchinson's eye increased the risk, but the stakes justified it. If that meant incurring collateral damage and taking more lives, then so be it.

He would do whatever the hell it took to save himself.

Chapter Five

Emily gave a happy sigh and smiled to herself as she picked up the glass antique cake pedestal. This was what Christmas was all about. Everyone was finally here, her home was filled with laughter and conversation, and now everyone she loved best was under the same roof.

Her heart was full to bursting as she carried her great-grandmother's famous coconut cake into the living room. Luke had lit a fire in the fireplace earlier, and combined with the glow of the decorated tree in the corner, the entire room felt festive and cozy.

"Ta-da," she announced, setting the cherished confection on the coffee table next to the stack of plates and forks Rayne had set out earlier in anticipation of his favorite dessert.

"I hope you made more than one," he said, eyeing the lone cake in concern.

She laughed. "Yes I did, greedy. Now. Ladies first." She cut a piece and handed it to Neveah with a smile. "Here you go, sweetie."

"Thanks." She turned her plate away protectively as

her husband, Rhys, tried to steal her fork for a bite. He and Ben were fraternal twins, and now Rhys was married too, after shocking everyone by popping the question to Neveah only a few months after their ordeal in Vancouver last November. "Wait your turn. Jeez."

"You too," Sam scolded Ben as Emily handed her a piece.

"But I've been looking forward to this all day," Ben protested.

"It's the best," Rayne said. "Make mine a big piece, will you?" he said to her.

"You're impossible." Emily grinned and kept dishing out cake, one piece for Christa and one for Bryn.

Today had been everything she'd hoped for and more. She was especially grateful for having everyone around to help take her mind off everything and ease her worry. A full house meant lots to keep her busy and her mind occupied, and that's just the way she preferred it. Wandering around with nothing to do made her feel lazy and useless. She much preferred staying busy and having a purpose.

"Just a small slice for me," Luke said when it was his turn.

"I'll share one with you," Emily said. Cancer loved to feed on sugar, but it was the holidays and she was allowing herself a piece.

"You're nuts," Ben said around a mouthful of cake. "This is wicked awesome."

"Try being over fifty, out of the field, and living with someone who bakes things made of butter and sugar at least three times a week," Luke answered wryly. "I love it, but I can't eat it like I used to."

"Oh, please," Emily said with a scoff. "You're still in incredible shape." As sexy as ever.

He quirked a dark eyebrow. "No thanks to you and your cooking."

She lowered the cake server and gave him a stunned look. "And here I thought I was partially responsible for helping you burn off the extra calories."

Everyone laughed except for Rayne, who grimaced. "Mom. Come on," he groaned. "Not in front of me."

Smiling, she finally handed him his extra-large piece. "There you go." She took a small one for herself and snuck in between Bryn and Luke on the tufted leather sofa next to the fire, then offered a bite to Luke, which he took.

Finally taking a bite herself, she sighed. Food held so many memories for her. One bite of the cake, and she was transported back in time to when this house belonged to her grandmother. Every special occasion they spent together, she and her grandmother had made this same cake, but especially at Christmas.

"What's that under the tree?" Luke said, looking over her shoulder.

Emily glanced back and saw the little parcel wrapped in shiny silver paper, decorated with a red satin bow. "I don't know." She glanced around at the others, and received blank looks. So she gave Luke a suspicious smile. "Did you put it there?"

He shook his head. "Not me."

She got up and went over to crouch down beside the tree. The extra strands of white lights Luke had strung on it made it easy to read the label. "It's to us, but it doesn't say who it's from." She looked around the room at the others, narrowing her eyes and giving them a playful smile. "So sneaky. Should I open it?"

"Definitely," said Bryn, forking another bite of cake into her mouth.

Bryn had been a trooper so far, even though it must be hard for her to be here with everyone while Dec was in harm's way somewhere overseas. Emily knew exactly what that was like, and made sure to spend lots of time

50

with her friend to keep her spirits up.

Picking up the gift, she carried it back to the sofa. Luke settled an arm around her shoulders as she undid the ribbon, then began rolling it up.

Ben groaned and set his fork down on his empty plate. "Oh, God, you're one of those too."

Sam elbowed him gently, laughing. "Not everyone is a savage like you when it comes to bows and wrapping paper," she chided him.

"It's meant to be torn off," he argued. "None of this trying to save the paper crap."

"I've always done it this way," Emily said, amused.

"You go, Em. You're doing it the right way," Sam said in encouragement.

"Thank you." Emily placed the rolled-up ribbon aside and carefully lifted the flap on one side of the wrapping paper.

"Seriously, why?" Ben asked. "You gonna reuse it on a gift the exact same size afterward? It makes no sense."

Emily laughed. "Maybe. Mostly I'm just enjoying getting a rise out of you for a change."

"That's my girl," Luke said, amusement in his deep voice.

A white paper box was revealed under the paper. Inside that, she found a blue velvet box closed with a fastener made of gold cording. She opened the lid, took out the exquisite glass tree ornament, and gasped.

"Merry Christmas to the grandparents-to-be—" Her head jerked up, her gaze shooting to Rayne and Christa in shock.

Her son stared at her blankly. Christa sat frozen with her fork poised partway to her mouth, and her eyes widened when she met Emily's gaze. "What? *No*. Not us. Definitely not us. I've got the Olympics coming up, remember? No baby on board here." She glanced questioningly at Sam and Bryn, seated on either side of her.

Emily smothered her momentary disappointment and looked at Sam, who waved her hands in front of her and shook her head. "Not us either."

She turned to Bryn next, who looked as stunned as Emily felt. "No, not me," Bryn said.

Then that only left...

As one, seven pairs of eyes turned to stare incredulously at Neveah and Rhys.

Rhys grinned and stretched a massive arm across his wife's shoulders as Neveah blushed and smiled. "Surprise," he said quietly.

The room erupted into happy chaos.

The women all cried out and jumped to their feet, and Ben shot from his seat to stare at his twin, his face full of shock. "You tight-lipped bastard, are you *kidding* me?" he said to Rhys, bending to grab his brother's hand and drag him to his feet. "Oh my God." He caught his twin in a bear hug, lifting the larger man off his feet a few inches in his enthusiasm, his booming, contagious laugh filling the room.

Rhys clapped his brother on the back, his almost embarrassed grin melting Emily's heart. "Yeah. Surreal, right?"

"Hell, yes. I'm gonna be an uncle."

"Yeah. Don't worry, you and Sam get an ornament too."

Ben put him down and drew his head back a little to scowl at him. "Can't believe you didn't tell me as soon as you found out."

Rhys shrugged. "We wanted to make it through the first trimester, and decided to surprise everyone at once."

"Do Mom and Dad know?"

"No, we're gonna surprise them the same way when we see them. So don't say anything, punk."

Ben grinned at the warning, then relented. "All right." Then he held his arms out to Neveah, who was currently engulfed in a group hug by all the women. "Come here, you."

Nev stepped into his embrace. She was tall, just under six feet, but even so she looked tiny next to the twins.

Emily's throat tightened, happy tears stinging her eyes as she clasped her hands to her chest. "A baby..."

"I didn't know you guys were even trying," Sam said as she wiped at her cheeks, a tremulous smile on her lips.

"We didn't try for very long," Nev said in a dry voice, shooting her husband an amused look. "The nerve damage in my hand means I still can't go back into the O.R., and so we decided waiting to start a family was kind of pointless. We just didn't expect it to happen so soon."

"When are we talking?" Ben asked.

"End of July."

Emily held out her arms for Rhys. "I'm so, so happy for you both." The couple had both stared death in the face and beaten the odds. They deserved every happiness together, and them having a baby was just too precious.

Rhys's hard face melted into another grin. He'd already smiled more in the past five minutes than he had in all the other times Emily had spent with him.

He stepped around the coffee table and engulfed her in those huge arms of his, holding her carefully, as if afraid he might break her if he squeezed too hard. "Thanks. So, will you guys be honorary grandparents?"

"Of course we will! Won't we, Luke?" She ducked her head to the side to see past Rhys to where her husband stood.

"Be honored to," Luke said, holding out a hand to Rhys. "Just as long as you don't expect me to do any diaper duty," he added as they shook.

Emily took the beautiful ornament over to the tree and carefully hung it on a branch front and center amongst all the other cherished keepsakes of Christmas past she'd held onto, making sure the lights shone on it just so.

Magic. That's what this holiday had been so far. Pure magic. "This is so exciting," she squealed, clapping her hands and bouncing on her toes.

"Yeah, and I'd personally like to thank you both for taking the pressure off us and giving my mom a grandbaby to fuss over," Rayne said next to Christa. "She's beside herself to be a grandma, but it'll be a few years for us yet."

"Not too many," Christa added with a secret smile that got Emily far too excited.

Going back to Luke, Emily leaned her head on his shoulder as he slung an arm around her waist. "We're gonna be grandparents," she murmured, choking up a little from the joy flooding her.

"Guess so," he said, kissing the top of her head in a way that made her heart squeeze.

The chime of his phone was barely audible above the conversation still buzzing around the room. He pulled it out of his pocket, glanced at it. "I gotta make a quick call. Be right back."

Before she could ask him what was going on, he'd already turned away and was striding from the room.

****

Dec McCabe hauled his gear from the belly of the C-130 and trudged down the tail ramp with his teammates. He was dead-ass tired after the late trans-Atlantic flight, but glad to be back on American soil, and looking forward to seeing his wife after being apart for the last six weeks.

Circumstances surrounding this latest mission meant he'd hardly been at base, so hadn't been able to call or email her much. He couldn't wait to surprise her by showing up in person soon.

As they crossed the tarmac toward the lit hangar, a lone silhouette stood waiting off to one side of the open bay door. Tall, big build, leaning on a cane.

"Well, look who it is," the man called out. "Lieutenant McCabe, still kickin'."

Dec grinned at that familiar voice, his buddy's face finally coming into view as he got closer. "Spencer." He dropped his stuff and grabbed the former medic in a bear hug, laughing. "How the hell are you, brother?"

"Still kickin' too. Only with one leg, of course," he joked.

The bullet Spencer had taken in the thigh while defending Bryn a couple years ago had cost him his career in the Teams, but the Navy refused to let him go and wanted to bring him on as an instructor here in Virginia Beach. "What the hell are you doing out here at this time of night?"

"Heard you and the boys were coming in. Thought I'd come down and say hello. You headed home tonight?"

"No, I'm headed down to Joint Base Charleston to surprise Bryn. She's staying with Hutchinson."

Spencer's sandy blond eyebrows hiked up. "That right? Give her a hug from me."

Dec smirked. "Not likely. Perv. You already kissed the hell out of her once." In the hospital in Beirut when he and Bryn had both been recovering from wounds sustained during the op to rescue her.

Spencer sobered. "No, seriously. I owe her."

"For?"

A smile tugged at his friend's lips. "I'm headed to Maine tomorrow."

Dec couldn't fathom why. "Why, what's up there?"

"Staying at a cabin with my lady."

Now it was Dec's turn to raise his eyebrows. "You off the market again?"

"Was never on it." A big smile spread across his face.

"Tara asked me to spend Christmas with her, just the two of us."

Dec's eyes widened in shock as he gripped his buddy's shoulder. Spencer and his wife had been on the verge of divorce for a few years now, though Spencer hadn't wanted it and still loved Tara as much as ever. But clearly something big had changed since Dec had last talked to him. "That's awesome, Spence. I'm happy for you. What happened?"

"It was Bryn's doing."

Dec stared at him, confused. "What do you mean?"

"She wrote Tara a letter about a year ago, pleading my case. Apparently they wrote back and forth for a while, and Tara finally called to talk to her early this fall. Whatever Bryn said, it made the difference, because Tara phoned me out of the blue a few weeks back. She says she misses me, and is willing to try and work things out."

Dec shook his head, floored. He knew Bryn cared about Spencer, that they'd bonded during the harrowing mission to rescue Bryn and her father. But he hadn't realized the lengths his wife was willing to go to in order to help his buddy. Damn, he loved her big heart.

"I didn't know." What other secrets had his wife kept from him?

Spencer shrugged. "I just found out about it myself." He shifted his stance, leaning more weight on the cane. "You got time for a beer before you head out?"

Dec glanced at his watch. "Yeah, man. Come on." He clapped his buddy on the back, grabbed his gear and walked with him into the hangar. When everything was squared away, they drove off base to a little bar and caught up over a cold one.

Just as they were finishing up, Dec's cell rang. He was surprised to see Luke's number. "Hutch. What's up?"

"You still OCONUS?"

"No, Virginia Beach. We got in a few days early, so

I'm actually catching a flight to Charleston in a bit. Don't tell Bryn, I wanna surprise her."

"Roger that. Listen, just wondered if you've been involved with anything pertaining to Said Kader."

Dec stilled at the name, thinking of the most recent failed op to capture him in Syria. He couldn't tell Luke about any of that, however, because the mission was classified and Luke was technically not with the Agency anymore, even with his security clearance.

"I know about him. Why?" They weren't on a secure line, either. Luke had to be damn concerned to talk about this so openly without one.

"I'm hearing from my contacts that he was killed in Idlib last week in a drone strike. You hear the same?"

Dec straightened up on the barstool, starting to get a little concerned himself. Either Luke's contact had bad intel, or he'd straight up lied. Both possibilities bothered Dec.

"No. In fact, that's the opposite of what I heard." They wouldn't have sent Dec and his boys to capture Kader if they thought he might be dead. The HVT was missing, and no one knew where the hell he was hiding now.

"Was afraid of that," he muttered.

"What's this about?" Dec asked, frowning.

Luke paused. "Someone sent Sam an encrypted list of accounts and transactions. All offshore. Whoever it is went to a lot of trouble to hide the money. We don't know who sent the intel or why. But there are pictures attached of an Agency officer I know, and Kader's in the background. I'm starting to think they were working together. At least when that picture was taken."

That didn't sound good, and it was news to Dec. They hadn't been told anything like this in any of the briefings on Kader. "When did she get the intel?"

"Yesterday afternoon."

"You talk to Jamie about it?" Luke's former boss.

"Not yet. He's away with his family for the holidays. I don't want to reach out until I've got a solid handle on what this is. When are you due in?"

"Oh-two-hundred or so."

"We'll talk more tomorrow. I'll leave the porch light on for you."

Chapter Six

Something was up. And he didn't like being left in the dark, especially where his twin was concerned.

Rhys waited until everyone else had gone upstairs to bed before cornering his brother in Luke's study with Sam. Ben looked up at him from next to her, the two of them huddled together looking at something on her laptop.

First, Luke had disappeared in here to make a call right after the baby announcement, then Ben and Sam had followed a while later. Rhys intended to find out what it meant. "What's going on?" he asked his twin.

"We don't really know, to be honest," Ben said. "Trying to unravel a mystery."

"What mystery?" Rhys walked over and stood behind them so he could see the laptop screen while Sam ran him through everything.

The more Sam said, the less Rhys liked it. Whatever this was, it involved an active duty paramilitary officer, and one of the country's most wanted terrorists. And someone had involved Sam, which made this personal.

She finished explaining everything with a little shrug. "If we find out who's been funneling money into these offshore accounts, we'll have a better idea of what we're dealing with."

"What about the note and the key?"

"Best we can tell it's coordinates, though we're not sure what the sender was trying to point us to. The area's an industrial-type place. Lots of warehouses, a few businesses and a couple storage places. The key could be for any of them, we'll have to keep digging on that one. Most places are closed for the holidays now. We can start calling around on the twenty-seventh if we don't find anything before then."

"Why didn't you report it to the Agency?"

"Luke is holding off on contacting Jamie until we have more information. And also, because of who we're dealing with, Luke thinks there might be some kind of Agency corruption involved. We won't report the evidence until we figure out what's really going on here," Ben said.

He absorbed that in silence, agreed that some caution was needed until they had more intel. At least he was satisfied that there was no imminent threat here. Yet. He relaxed his posture. "You reached out to any personal contacts about this yet?"

"Luke did the other night, to a guy not with the Agency anymore," Ben answered, chewing away on his Big Red. "He was told Kader was killed in a drone strike last week, but Dec says no. Anyway, we'll all feel better when we start to get some answers."

Him too. Sam was his sister now, and if this whole thing put her in any sort of danger, he would do whatever he could to help keep her safe. "Just tell me what you need done, and I'll do it."

Sam smiled at him warmly. "You're so sweet, thank you."

Rhys grunted, the back of his neck warming. Sweet was only something Nev and his mother said about him.

Ben tipped back in his chair, put his hands behind his head and grinned at him. "You're gonna be a father. That's wicked awesome. I still can't believe it."

A smile tugged at Rhys's own lips. "Yeah, I know."

"How's Nev feeling, anyway?" Sam asked, fingers poised over the keyboard. "Has she been sick?"

"Not too bad, and she's getting better every day. First trimester's over in another few days." Then they could both breathe a bit easier.

Though when he thought about having a newborn handed to him, it made him break out in a cold sweat. He knew shit about caring for a baby, and prayed he had some kind of paternal instinct hidden away inside that would magically spring to life when the baby came.

Ben nodded at the door. "Well, what are you standing here talking to us for? Better go up and take care of her."

Rhys didn't mind the dismissal, because upstairs with Nev was exactly where he wanted to be now that he wasn't worried about a dangerous situation going down here. "See you in the morning."

The house was still and quiet as he made his way up the carpeted runner on the curved staircase to the second floor. The guest room he and Nev were staying in was at the far end of the upstairs hall. Emily had given them the king-size bed, which he appreciated because he and Nev were both tall, and squeezing into a double or even a Queen bed made for an uncomfortable sleeping situation.

A strip of light spread out from under the door onto the hardwood floor of the hallway. He opened the door a few inches, checking to see if she was asleep. Nev was sitting up against the headboard of the four-poster, canopied bed, reading.

She set her e-reader down on her lap and smiled. "Hi."

He came in and shut the door, feeling totally out of

place in the soft yellow, feminine room. "Hi."

God, she was so beautiful amongst all that pale yellow bedding, her arms and upper chest bare beneath the straps of her nightie. Her dark brown hair fell all loose and shiny in waves around her shoulders, and her sapphire blue eyes were filled with warmth as she watched him. "Feeling okay?"

"Yeah, just tired. You?"

His eyebrows went up. "Me? I'm fine." Better now that he knew what was going on with Ben and Sam. His twin might irritate the shit out of him sometimes, but there was nothing Rhys wouldn't do for him and Sam.

Nev gave a low chuckle as he approached the bed. "That was a whole lotta emoting all at once for you earlier. Bet you're as tired as I am now."

He half-smirked and started stripping, laying his clothes over the dainty chair in the corner of the room. It looked like it would break if he tried to sit on it. "I'm getting better."

"You were already pretty great to begin with," she told him, her gaze sweeping over the length of his naked body and back up again. "I've got no complaints."

When she looked at him like that, with pride and pure female admiration, his ego swelled. Along with another part of him that needed to chill the hell out right now. She was three months pregnant, and tired.

"Glad to hear it." He climbed in next to her, froze when the antique bedframe gave an ominous creek. Shit, he didn't want to break the bed.

Nev laughed softly and sat up to wind her arms around him from behind, her palms pressed to his bare chest. The feel of her breasts pressed to his back sent more blood rushing to his groin. "Now that would be funny, trying to explain how the bed just broke without us even doing anything."

He huffed out a laugh and gingerly stretched out next

to her on his back. The wooden frame creaked, but there was no popping or cracking. "I'll just lie here like this and not move all night."

"Mmm, that gives me so many tantalizing ideas," she murmured, rolling on top of him.

He grabbed her hips to still her when the bed groaned, freezing in place. Afraid to breathe. This bed had probably been in Emily's family for over a hundred years. He didn't want to be the one to wreck it.

Nev's shoulders shook with silent laughter, then she came up on her elbows to peer down at him, her gorgeous hair falling around them like a soft curtain. "Hi." She traced a finger down the side of his cheek.

He was rock hard against her abdomen as he smoothed a hand up the silky length of her back, then down to the cool satin covering her beautifully curved ass. Raising his head from the pillow, his heart swelled when she met him partway, her lips melding with his. She sighed and nestled her head against his shoulder, smothering a yawn.

Reminded of how tired she was, Rhys ignored his hopeful erection and carefully rolled her to her side, turning her away from him before pulling her in tight to his body. He ran his left hand over the length of her arm, then down to cradle the tiny swell of her abdomen where their baby was curled up deep inside her. Man, it still floored him.

"Ben was pretty excited, huh?" she murmured. "So sweet."

"Yeah." Little punk had always been the more emotional and demonstrative of the two of them. Rhys actually liked that about him. "He's going to be an awesome uncle."

She laid her hand on top of his, her fingers caressing the back of it. "And you're going to be a fantastic dad."

"Hope so."

She angled her face toward him. "What's that mean? You're gonna be great."

He made a sound of agreement, but deep down he worried about that. She knew his background. Though they were twins, he'd been kind of a father figure to Ben in a way, but he hadn't known what a proper parental figure was until their adopted parents stepped in.

For their formative years, he and Ben had pretty much been left to their own devices on the streets of south Boston. They'd been in survival mode for most of their childhood, and it had shaped their personalities well before they'd been put into the foster system. It was the reason why Rhys still struggled to allow himself to feel and express strong emotion.

Neveah wouldn't let it go. She rolled to face him, her eyes troubled in the soft lamplight as she studied him. "What is it?"

He let out a breath. Talking about shit still wasn't in his top hundred favorite things to do, but if she really wanted to know, he'd tell her. All except the part where he confessed he was worried about her, that something would go wrong during the pregnancy or birth. He needed to keep that to himself.

"I guess I… I just want our baby to have the opposite of my childhood." Rhys didn't want their child to know hunger or fear or shame like he and Ben had. He wanted the baby to be healthy, happy, and most of all, *safe*.

Her expression softened. "This baby is going to have an incredible childhood, and an amazing life. He or she will be protected, never go hungry, and never go a day without feeling loved or secure."

He nodded and drew her head to his shoulder so she couldn't keep staring at him. His life hadn't been easy, and even after the Sinclairs had stepped in and stabilized his and Ben's lives years ago, something had been missing for him.

He'd gone into the military right after high school and eventually made it into The Unit, then spent most of his adult life doing things most people couldn't imagine. He'd taken so many lives. It seemed unbelievable that he was about to bring one into the world. Part of him felt like he didn't deserve that chance after everything he'd done.

"And I can hear your brain working from here, so I'm gonna stop you right there, because in spite of what you may think about yourself, you have an incredible amount of love to give our baby," Nev told him, intuitively knowing what was going on in his head. "You being an elite soldier just means you'll be that much more capable of protecting our baby. I know you still worry that part of you is dead inside, but that's just not true. Know how I know?"

"How?" he said to placate her, though he was secretly hanging on her every word.

"Because of the way you love me and your family. That's all the proof you need, right there." She ran a hand over his chest, her touch soothing him deep inside, smoothing over all the jagged pieces he tried to hide from the world. Even from Nev, whom he loved with his whole heart.

"I know the thought of being a parent," she continued, "of being responsible for a tiny life that depends on us is kinda scary. I never thought much about being a mother either, until after what happened in Vancouver. But you know what? You and I have what it takes."

"You're gonna be an incredible mother," he murmured against her hair. Nev was strong, bold, and she also had one of the biggest hearts of anyone he'd ever met.

She'd risked her life to offer medical help to the poorest people in war-torn countries with Doctors Without Borders. She'd been taken captive because of it, and had survived everything fate threw at her, including being locked in that elevator with a knife-wielding madman.

She still bore the scars from it, and he loved and admired her all the more for being a survivor.

Nev's soft smile turned his heart over. "I can't wait."

Rhys wrapped his fingers around her wrist and brought it to his mouth, kissing the surgical scar that had marked the end of her career and the chance to begin this next phase of their life together. She was ecstatic about becoming a mother, and not the least bit worried that anything would go wrong. She amazed him. "I love you."

Her eyes were filled with tenderness and understanding. "Love you back. And it's going to be okay, I promise." She kissed him softly, then took his hand and settled her palm flat over her abdomen before snuggling into him.

Rhys reached behind him and turned off the reading lamp. Tucking his wife against him, he thought about what she'd just said. Of everything they'd faced together until now, and the future that lay ahead of them.

Everything *would* be okay, because Rhys would make sure of it.

He just hoped he could live up to Nev's expectations and be the kind of father their child deserved.

Chapter Seven

Bryn woke in the middle of a dream when the bed dipped suddenly. She inhaled a sharp breath and came up on one elbow just as a large silhouette came into view beside her. Her heart rocketed up her throat.

"Merry Christmas," a deep voice murmured.

She froze in surprise, the fear vanishing in an instant as her heart settled back where it belonged. "Dec!" She flung her arms around him and buried her face in the side of his neck, his deep chuckle reverberating in his chest as he crushed her to him. Reassuring her that she wasn't dreaming.

"Surprise."

She hugged him tight, joy flooding her. "When did you get back?" He smelled like sweat but she didn't care. She hadn't heard from him in almost two weeks, and hadn't expected to see him for another few at least. Their most recent mission must have either flopped, or gone really well.

"Landed in Virginia Beach a few hours ago, then hopped a flight down here." He nuzzled her hair, his big hands sliding over her naked back. "I need a shower. You wanna join me?"

"Only if I get to wash you."

"Oh, that goes without saying." He tipped her head back and kissed her gently, then tugged her from the bed and into the en suite. She squinted as he flipped on the light, then anxiously ran her gaze over him.

Dec reached past her to start the shower, then she turned him around to face the sink and inspected the back of him too. "What are you doing?" he asked.

"Just making sure you're really okay."

He met her gaze in the mirror, his golden eyes filled with amusement. "You don't trust that I'd tell you if I wasn't?"

"No." He was a SEAL. Suffering in silence was part of their code. Her least favorite part.

He grinned and captured her hands, bringing them to his mouth for a kiss, his dark stubble rasping against her skin. "Missed you, baby."

She flattened herself against his back, savoring every point of contact. "Missed you more."

Waiting for her warrior to return never got any easier, even when he was just away for training. Some days dragged by, and while she tried not to obsess over the news about what was going on in various hot spots around the world when he was away, she couldn't avoid it completely. She never knew where he was, and he couldn't tell her, though she could make an educated guess.

But now he was here, and everything else fell away.

When the water was hot, Dec stepped under the spray and tugged her in after him. One arm locked around her waist as his other hand slid into her hair, his mouth coming down on hers. Bryn wound her arms around his neck and melted into his kiss, her tongue gliding along his as she ran her hands over that gorgeous, powerful body she'd missed so damn much.

She grabbed the soap from the shelf in the corner and

began rubbing it all over him in slow circles, covering him with slippery lather while his hands roamed over her naked body. By the time she made it down between his legs, he was hard and ready for her.

She hummed in appreciation and stroked him, slow and firm, adding a little swirl with her fist as she reached the sensitive head. Dec growled into her mouth and spun them around, pinning her to the tile wall before dipping his head to take an aching nipple into his mouth.

Bryn gasped and rubbed her swelling folds against the rock-hard length of his erection, her body tingling all over, clit throbbing. His hands held her steady as he sucked on her sensitive flesh, sending delicious currents of sensation spiraling through her.

After giving the same attention to her other nipple, he dropped to one knee, gripped her calf and lifted her leg over his shoulder, parting her slick folds for the intimate caress of his tongue. Bryn held her breath, her heart racing, anticipating the first silken caress of that talented tongue.

When it came, she plunged her fingers into his thick hair, her back arching as she bit her lip to stop a shuddering moan. This was an old house. The walls were thin. And Dec was a generous lover. He paid attention to the details, including every tiny pleasure point on her body.

Her eyes slid closed, a shudder speeding through her muscles as his tongue caressed her. *Ohh, Dec...*

She'd missed him. Missed just having him around, having him close, and dear God, yes, she'd missed *this*. Being able to touch him, and have his hands and mouth on her again.

He knew exactly what spot felt best, knew exactly what pressure and speed she liked. It felt like she was melting against his tongue, his strong hands holding her hips steady, the only thing keeping her on her feet while pleasure coursed through her.

She was breathing fast, all swollen and needy when he stroked his tongue across her clit one last time, then surged to his feet. Before she could protest, he spun her around to brace her forearms on the tile, and pulled her hips back toward him.

Bryn parted her legs and arched her ass toward him, arousal rocketing through her as she looked over her shoulder at him. His face was set, his eyes burning with need as he reached down to position the head of his cock between her folds.

She closed her eyes, gasped a moment later when a continuous stream of warm water pulsed over her throbbing clit. She opened her eyes and looked down to find him angling the detachable shower wand between her legs. With a smile and a hum of pleasure she rested her cheek against the cool tile and pressed back toward the hot, tantalizing pressure of him lodged against her.

The flow of water was warm and decadent, giving her just the right stimulation to start her on the climb to release. Then Dec surged into her with a single, controlled thrust that made her clench around him, a moan tearing free in spite of her efforts to keep quiet.

She needed him. Needed him to ease this ache inside her. To give her the release she craved and then hold her tight in bed for the rest of the night. The long separations and uncertainty while he was gone were always hard.

"God, I've missed being inside you," he whispered against the side of her neck. His free hand came up to play with a hard nipple as he eased his hips back and gave another slow thrust that buried him deep.

Yes. "Just like that," she gasped out. "Don't stop."

He groaned. "Love it when you clench around my cock."

The pressure of the water rushing over her clit was perfect, his slow, smooth rhythm hitting just the right place inside her as he pushed her up, up, the orgasm already building. "Dec," she moaned, her hands fisting against the tile, eyes squeezing shut.

"Yeah, baby, come all over my cock," he rasped out.

There was no way she could stop it. The orgasm hit, pulsing through her in wave after delicious wave while she shuddered and stifled her moans.

Slowly the pleasure ebbed away. The water on her clit became too much. She pushed his hand away and leaned her weight into the wall, panting.

Behind her, Dec nipped the curve of her neck, gripped her hips hard, and drove in and out of her deeper. A little harder.

She reached back to cup the back of his head and moved with him as he rode her to his own release. His big body shuddered as he drove deep and locked there, his guttural moan of ecstasy smothered against the side of her neck.

Bryn shivered in the sudden chill and realized the water was now spraying on her feet. She caught the now dangling shower wand and reached up to slide it back into place. They both sighed as the warm water cascaded over them once more, Dec's heavy body still pressing her to the wall.

He kissed the curve of her shoulder and wrapped his arms around her waist, drawing her back against the warmth of his chest. They stayed like that for a few minutes, coming back to earth together under the flowing water.

"I'm so glad you're here," Bryn murmured finally. *So glad you're safe.*

"Me too." He withdrew gently, then turned her to face him and stroked some wet hair away from her cheek, one steely arm coiling around her waist. "I love you."

Her lips curved. "Love you too." She kissed him, lips and tongue lingering, hungry for more of this incredible connection she'd only ever felt with him.

71

Dec raised his head to smile at her. "Got to see Spencer at the base, by the way. He sends his love."

She tipped her head back to look into his face. God, he was beautiful. "How is he?"

"Great." He nuzzled the side of her face. "Didn't know you were playing cupid behind the scenes."

She smiled at his teasing tone. "I couldn't stand them not trying one last time at least. Tara just needed to see what he's like when he's working. And since I had firsthand experience with that..."

"You're such a romantic."

She hummed, not bothering to deny it. "Why do you think I fell for you? And by the way, we're gonna be an honorary aunt and uncle in the summer."

He stilled. "You're kidding. Who?"

"Rhys and Nev."

His golden eyes widened. "No shit?"

"No. It was pretty adorable when they told us. Everyone was shocked. I think Ben's the most excited of all."

Dec searched her eyes. He was so strong, loyal and brave, it turned her heart over. "What about you? Think you're ready for that too?"

They'd talked about trying for a baby soon. She'd always loved kids. It was a big reason why she'd become a social worker in the first place. She definitely wanted to be a mother, even if it meant doing some parts of it on her own for now because of Dec's demanding training and deployment schedule.

"I think so. And I also think trying for a baby could be a lot of fun." She grinned and kissed his bristly chin. "So, how long do I have you for, anyway?" She squeezed his naked butt.

He cocked a dark eyebrow. "How long do you want me?"

"Pretty sure you already promised me forever."

He grinned, revealing the twin dimples in his dark-stubbled cheeks. "Yeah, I did, didn't I? Guess that means you're stuck with me."

She wished she got to be stuck with him more often. And she was already dreading the moment he left again.

Chapter Eight

Joe lowered his phone to watch the live video one of his guys was shooting near White Point Gardens, at the southern tip of the Battery in Charleston. Hutchinson and his wife lived only a couple blocks from it. The man taking the surveillance video was posing as a runner out for a morning jog, his phone clipped to his fanny pack.

The camera bounced up and down with every stride, but the shot was clear enough. Ancient, towering oak trees filled the park. Beyond it out in Charleston Harbor sat the infamous island stronghold of Fort Sumter, where the first shots of the Civil War had been fired. If all went according to plan, Joe would see the historic site in person later tonight once it was empty.

Its position in the middle of the harbor was perfect for his purposes, because it would take anyone coming after them longer to organize and get out there. It was also large enough to accommodate his exfil plan.

The last tour of the day left Liberty Square at fourteen-thirty-hours. By the time Joe got there with his prisoner it would be empty except for the two rangers on shift. It would be a simple matter to deal with them and the fort's security cameras.

His scout crossed South Battery, the main road running alongside the park. The residential streets here were quieter, the sidewalks lining historic homes that had been there for centuries. Joe knew every inch of this street from studying it on satellite images, but to get good intel on his target he needed a live shot to find out for certain if she was there.

Samarra and Ben Sinclair had arrived in Charleston two days ago. Guaranteed she would have done something with the information she'd received by now. Credit card records pointed to a specific rental car agency, and Joe had been able to find the make, model and plate number of the vehicle they'd rented. A few pings of the plate number had led him here, and within moments Joe would know if his suspicions had been correct.

The runner turned right and headed up a side street, lined with magnolias and palmettos. Joe watched intently as a familiar black wrought iron gate appeared off to the side, and a stately brick mansion with white pillars came into view. The runner turned up the alley running behind the house, where cars were parked against the curb.

And sure enough, there was the Sinclairs' rental vehicle.

Joe picked up a burner phone and contacted his crew. *Target located. Take positions now.*

He had six guys with him on this op. Might seem like overkill just to capture one woman, but Hutchinson and Samarra's husband had served in elite military units. Joe wasn't taking any chances, and wasn't about to attack the house, where they were all together.

He had something else in mind. All he needed was to find the right opportunity to split them up. When his team executed this op, it had to be all shock and awe, catching their prey unawares.

Another of his burners rang. One of his men calling.

"Yeah?"

"You're gonna love this. Hutchinson's got a full house right now. I can't get an ID on anyone yet, but there's at least eight people in there, maybe more. And Tim managed to trace a cell call from the house to a local tour company a few minutes ago. We called there to check, and Hutchinson's wife apparently signed five of them up for a walking history tour tonight. All women."

A shot of adrenaline punched through him. "Was Samarra's name on the list?"

"Yes."

His pulse sped up, a plan already forming in his mind. Samarra would be there, undefended. This is exactly the break he'd needed. "What time is the tour?"

"Leaves at five from Liberty Square, but they have to check in twenty minutes prior."

Right near the water, where the ferry took tourists out to the fort. It was perfect. "I'm on it. Tell the others to hold their positions. I'll contact everyone with orders within the next few hours."

He ended the call and immediately pulled up a map of the area, coordinating everything in his mind. Without the location of that storage unit, he was screwed. If this next op failed, he was screwed.

But he had no choice. He had to act, and he had to act now, because he wasn't going down without a fight.

He would take Samarra, and do whatever was necessary to force her to give him what he needed to find that storage unit, staving off disaster.

****

Sam muttered to herself as she pored over the notes she'd compiled. Finding out who an offshore company was registered to was a lot more difficult than one might think. And if she dug too deep, she risked triggering a security alert and maybe even tipping off whoever was behind all this. So she had to be careful.

"Well, fancy finding you here."

She looked up at Ben as he came into the study carrying a mug and a plate of something that smelled so good it made her mouth water. "Ooh, what is it?" He'd still been asleep when she'd snuck down here to work.

"Bacon, and eggs Benedict with crab, shrimp and homemade hollandaise."

"Yum, thanks." She took the plate, her stomach rumbling. "Emily made all this already?"

Amusement gleamed in his pale eyes as he set her coffee down on the desk in front of her. "You've been in here for over two hours already."

She blinked and glanced at the clock on her laptop. "I have?"

"You have." He handed her a fork. "Eat up."

She cut herself a bite, and the creamy hollandaise with the fresh egg and crabmeat made her moan. "Oh, God, I'd gain so much weight if I lived here."

"Nah, I'd make sure I helped you burn it all off." His eyes held a wicked gleam.

She gave him a playful, quelling look, but it was spoiled by him ducking down and kissing her. And he didn't stop there, nibbling his way across her cheek and down the side of her neck while his hands moved down to cup her breasts, his thumbs gliding across the sensitive centers.

"Missed you this morning," he murmured in a husky voice that heated her insides.

She grabbed his wrists to stop his distracting fingers, kissed his jaw and pushed him away, flustered. Jeez, someone could walk in here at any moment and see them making out. "You just said you want me to eat."

His gaze glittered with unmistakable hunger as he looked down at her. "And I'd like to eat *you*. Missed you this morning when I woke up all alone in that fancy bed."

Oh, man. He made it so hard to concentrate when he got all smoldery and seductive like this. "I wanted to keep going on this," she told him, trying to ignore the hum of arousal he'd started deep in her belly. She had to get to the bottom of this. Sex could wait. "I feel like I'm close to cracking this thing." It was driving her nuts not knowing who'd sent the letter to her or why.

"I'll help," he murmured, leaning in to kiss her neck again, his lips lingering on the one spot there guaranteed to make her eyes cross.

She let out a squeak and pushed at his wide shoulders. "You're impossible. Quit distracting me."

He lifted his head to grin at her. "But I love distracting you."

"Don't I know this," she said with a mock scowl. She pushed at his shoulders again. Gah. So wide and full of muscle. She couldn't think when he turned on the seductive charm. "Go. Find something to amuse yourself with for a while longer, and then I'll finish up. Something that's not me," she added when she saw the mischievous twinkle in his eyes.

He sighed as if crushed and got to his feet. "Fine. I know when I'm not wanted."

Oh, she wanted him. That's why he needed to leave. She shook her head at him as he walked away, grabbing something from the shelf, then pausing to give her a pouty look as he slid the pocket door shut.

"That man," she muttered under her breath. "He's lucky I love him so much." Shoving another bite of breakfast into her mouth, she started tinkering more with the information she'd found.

Within an hour, she had what she'd been looking for. Only she didn't like the answer. Not one bit.

Stomach tight, she picked up her empty plate and carried it into the kitchen. Luke was doing dishes in the sink, and Emily was making something else at the island. "Thanks for breakfast, it was amazing," she said to Emily.

"You're welcome, and glad you liked it. Sleep okay?"

"Slept great." A lie, since she'd lain awake for hours turning everything over in her mind. Her gaze slid to Luke, who had his back to her. Before she could get his attention, Emily spoke again. "So, is it just us ladies tonight for the historic ghost tour?" Sam was looking forward to it.

"Yes, and I'm actually glad, because now we can enjoy ourselves without having a bunch of bored, long faces around."

Sam laughed. "Well, Luke and Rhys would have bored, long faces, but Ben would love it. He can have fun anywhere, I swear." Maybe that's why they worked so well as a couple. They balanced out each other's polar opposite personality.

"Now that I believe. Can you grab me the cinnamon from that cupboard over there?" She pointed to the one left of the range, one hand still mixing whatever was in the big bowl in front of her.

"Sure." Sam walked over and opened the cupboard. She grabbed the cinnamon, then turned and handed it to Em.

Em took it, then frowned, staring at the label. "What the…"

Looking over her shoulder, Sam read the white label stuck across the original one. *Ground Tree Bark.*

She gasped, her gaze shooting back to the open cupboard. Sure enough, there were more little white labels on a few other spice jars, all lined up in a row on the shelf.

I'm a Big Dill.
Oregano Gangsta.
It's Go Thyme.
I Beg Your Parsley.

And finally, the coup de grace. *I Wanna Cumin Your*—

Sam gasped and snatched that one from the shelf, whirling as she put it behind her back to hide it from Emily's view.

"What is it?" Emily asked.

Sam's face flushed. "Ben," she growled, glaring up at the ceiling because he was on the other side of it. Really? Again with the label maker thing? He must have grabbed it from the shelf in Luke's study to amuse himself with.

"Sorry," she said to Emily. "It's a thing he likes to do. Teasing me about my penchant for organizing stuff. I'll scrape them off."

"No, leave them. They're cute," Emily said, laughing.

Yeah, cute. She couldn't fault Ben for his wit, but that last one was way off the inappropriate scale for someone as ladylike as Emily.

"Oh, you're finished working?" his deep voice said behind her.

She turned to give her husband a hard stare. "Had fun amusing yourself while you waited, did you?"

"What?" he asked, all innocence as he came up to her. "You told me to find something to amuse myself with, other than you. So I did."

"You've really got to let the label thing go."

He grinned and kissed her, tickling her ribs and making her squawk and squirm. It was impossible to stay irritated with him. "But it's so fun. Did you see the cumin one?"

"I saw it. Are you ever going to grow up?" She was failing miserably at staying annoyed, and at not laughing from his tickles.

"Not if I can help it. And you're serious enough for the both of us."

That was true. "You mean I'm the more *adult* of the two of us."

"Sure." He gave her a smacking kiss on the lips and hugged her to him, squeezing tight, then put his mouth to her ear. "If you're done, does that mean I can get you alone upstairs for a while?" he whispered. "Because I really wanna cumin your—"

"Shh!" she hissed, aghast. Emily and Luke were both staring at them. "I found something," she blurted.

At that he straightened and met her gaze, dropping his teasing demeanor. "What is it?"

She caught Luke's gaze over by the sink. "You should see too."

Luke set the dishtowel down and gave Emily a warning look. "Be back in a minute, so don't you dare touch these dishes. I'll finish them when we're done."

Sam and Ben followed him into the study where Ben had put the label maker back on the shelf. "I got a name on the accounts," she told them as soon as Ben slid the door shut behind them.

"Who is it?" Luke asked, hands on hips.

"Joseph Hanes. And I'm guessing he doesn't get paid that kind of money on his government salary. From what I can tell, he's been embezzling what's probably dirty money from the American government, and someone wanted to expose him."

The question was, what were they going to do with the information now?

Chapter Nine

"Oh, that last house was the best of all," Sam said, slinging an arm around Emily's shoulders as they, Nev, Christa and Bryn all walked along the sidewalk toward the visitor's center at the end of their two-hour tour.

The historic Christmas walking ghost tour had been even more fun than she'd expected. She'd learned lots of interesting things, and the historic district was gorgeous, especially done up with holiday decorations.

"You just liked the mulled wine," Bryn said wryly.

"Yeah, because it was *awesome*." She was definitely tipsy. She'd had three cups of the warm, spiced perfection. "The tour guide loved the additions to the tour."

"Helps that Em knows pretty much everyone in this part of town," Bryn said. "Otherwise we wouldn't have been able to see inside any of the houses."

"The decorating was unreal," Christa added. "I've been dying to see inside these places since I first came down here, and to see the private gardens."

"I liked the treats," Nev said, polishing off the final shortbread she'd snagged from the last house.

"Good, because you're eating for two now," Emily

said.

Sam couldn't remember the last time she'd had this much fun. Hanging out with the girls had been awesome. "Hey, you guys wanna do some caroling?" she asked brightly.

The others all looked at her. "No," Nev said, laughing. "How 'bout you sing for Ben when he comes to get us?"

"I'm not gonna sing by myself," Sam grumbled. "I haven't had *that* much wine."

"You had yours *and* Nev's," Emily teased, then glanced at her watch. "Luke and Rayne should be on the way to pick us up," she said to Christa and Bryn. They needed two vehicles to get everyone back to the house. "I've got the games all ready to go."

"Mind if we make a quick pit stop first?" Nev asked as the visitor's center came into view. "One of the joys of pregnancy is having to go to the bathroom a billion times a day."

"I'll go with you," Em offered. "Menopause is the same."

"We'll wait for you on the sidewalk out front," Christa said, and the three of them kept going when Em and Nev peeled off to hit the bathroom.

"Where do you think Ben and Rhys went off to, anyway?" Bryn asked Sam as they passed the visitor's center. She wanted to come back tomorrow and tour the exhibit about Fort Sumter. People booked tours and took a ferry from nearby to go visit it.

"No idea, but I guarantee Ben's irritating the hell out of Rhys right now," Sam said, grinning. Things were never dull with Ben around.

Christa laughed. "I love the way they banter. You can tell they're close."

Sam nodded, feeling the tiniest bit dizzy. Or maybe it was because the sidewalk was uneven. "They're

83

ridiculous. Loyal to each other to the bitter end, though."

They stopped on the far sidewalk running along the main road in front of the visitor's center. Sam tipped her head back to stare up into the sky, inhaling even as she wobbled a bit. If she didn't fall asleep by the time they got back to the house, Ben was so getting lucky.

"It's so gorgeous out." An almost full moon hung in the dark blue sky, the breeze holding the salty scent of the nearby water as it rustled the palmetto fronds above them.

Rapid footsteps made her glance to her left. No sooner had she spotted the large silhouette coming at them than an arm snaked around her waist from behind.

A hard hand over her mouth stifled her cry of warning, and then two more men converged on Christa and Bryn. Before she could twist around to fight, something hard jabbed into her ribs.

She froze, her blood icing over at the feel of the gun pressed to her.

"Scream and you'll regret it," a deadly male voice growled in her ear.

CHRISTA'S HEART SHOT into her throat when a man materialized out of nowhere and grabbed Sam.

She opened her mouth to scream, instinctively turning to reach for Bryn, but someone grabbed her from behind, jerking her to a halt. A muscled arm locked around her waist, and a hard hand covered her mouth.

Instinct took over.

She sank her teeth into the hand over her mouth and whirled, momentarily breaking the man's grip. "Get away from me!" She lashed out with her foot, managed to catch him in the knee, making him stumble.

She'd been assaulted and kidnapped before. Never again.

She twisted around, terror forking through her. Bryn and Sam were both being dragged toward the road.

Behind her, she could hear the man she'd kicked coming after her.

Christa turned and ran down the sidewalk, yelling for help.

An SUV sped up to the curb in front of her, its headlights off, and plunged to a halt. She spun to the left, veering away from it. She could hear the running footsteps behind her, her pursuer coming closer.

Her skin prickled. "Help!" she screamed, and glanced over her shoulder.

The guy holding Sam was already dragging her toward the vehicle, and Bryn was struggling valiantly against her attacker.

A hand shot toward her. Christa wrenched away and spun hard, then sprinted for the hedge lining the sidewalk. But the guy chasing her was right behind her. Too close.

She hurdled the hedge, her heart slamming in her chest as she raced back toward the visitor's center. Nev and Emily. Were they okay? She had to attract attention and get help.

A strong hand caught the back of her jacket. She let out a scream and shrugged out of it, almost tripping before she regained her balance and kept running.

The man chasing her cursed, his closeness sending a rush of terror down her spine. *No!* He was right on top of her. She'd never be able to outrun him, and the visitor's center entrance was still too far away.

Her gaze landed on a hefty branch lying on the ground under a tree. She ducked to snag it as she ran, but her legs felt wobbly, the fear sapping her muscles and slowing her down.

The man behind her was right there, an arm's length away. Any second, he would grab her. She had to fight him off. She was Sam and Bryn's only chance to get help.

Gripping the end of the branch in both hands like a bat, she stopped suddenly and whirled to face her attacker, swinging it with every ounce of her strength.

The dry wood slammed across the side of the man's head, and shattered. He grunted, grabbing at his head as he fell sideways into the bushes.

Skin crawling, Christa dropped the branch and ran, but he was already up and after her again. The sidewalk ahead was empty.

"Help! Someone help me!" she screamed, hoping someone would hear her. There was no time to pull out her phone, she couldn't slow down.

She could hear the man's breaths as he chased after her, didn't risk a glance over her shoulder to see if he was unsteady on his feet. It sounded like he was getting closer with every heartbeat.

No! She had to stop him. Couldn't let him catch her.

She veered left, heard him curse and then the rustling of shrubs. She kept running, not daring to look back, but she'd just gained a few seconds' lead-time.

But he was still back there. Still coming after her. And the sidewalk ahead of her was still deserted. No one was coming to help her.

She glanced around frantically as she ran. The landscaping bordering the sidewalk transitioned from shrubs and hedges to round stones. Without pause she reached down to grab a softball-sized one, then planted her feet and whirled.

He was barely thirty feet away. Coming right at her.

Adrenaline pouring through her, she reared back her right arm and launched the rock at his face. She missed by inches.

She snatched up another stone, spun, and hurled it at him.

A sickening thud sounded as it slammed into his forehead. This time he went down hard, but she didn't wait to see if he got up, just spun and ran, her lungs about to explode.

Another hedge appeared in front of her. She leaped over it, her legs growing rubbery under the lash of terror, but then she was in front of the visitor's center at last.

Except there was no one there.

Swallowing a sob, she yanked her phone from her pocket and raced ahead for the bathroom, hoping to save Emily and Nev.

****

"I swear my bladder's already been reduced to the size of a damn walnut," Nev said as she did up her jeans and exited the washroom stall. The tour had been fun. Watching Sam get half-tanked had been even better.

Emily was already over at the sink washing her hands, and met her gaze in the mirror. "I remember what that was like. And enjoy those jeans while they still fit. It'll be a long while before you'll be in them again."

"I'm actually looking forward to wearing stretchy pants."

"How are you feeling, by the way? Any nausea or anything?"

"Some, though usually just if I go too long without eating." Nev soaped and washed her hands, noting the carefully concealed shadows beneath Emily's eyes. And if Nev wasn't mistaken, she'd lost some weight since they'd seen each other at the double wedding in August. "What about you, how are you feeling?"

Emily shot her a surprised look, then softened it with a smile. "Good. Loving every moment of having all of us together."

Now that Nev could believe. There wasn't a kinder soul on this earth than Emily, and she was a gracious and warm hostess. Nev would talk to Luke alone when she got the chance over the next day or two. If something was going on with Emily's health, he would tell her.

"We're loving it too." She accepted the paper towel Emily handed her.

"Good. And that surprise you pulled off last night was just incredible. I'm so excited to be an honorary meemaw." Emily pitched the used paper towel into the trashcan.

Nev laughed. "Is that what you want the baby to call you?"

"Of course, and Luke will be pawpaw."

Oh, she bet Luke was gonna *love* that. "Then meemaw and pawpaw it is." They started for the door.

"Is Rhys excited? He's still hard for me to read."

"Yes, but he's nervous."

"That's to be expected for any first-time daddy. But he'll do fine. Luke was amazing when Rayne was tiny, and he dealt with the sleep deprivation a thousand times better than me."

The thought of seeing Rhys, her hard, giant warrior husband, holding their newborn, was enough to turn her into mush. "That's good to hear." Not that she had any doubts about Rhys. He just needed some confidence about being a parent.

They stepped out into the cool night air. Nev glanced down the sidewalk in the direction the others had gone earlier. "Do you think—"

"Help!"

Nev's gaze shot to the left. She stiffened in alarm as Christa ran toward them, eyes wide, her face a mask of terror. "What's wrong?" she blurted, stepping out in front of her and glancing around defensively.

Christa stopped in front of them and bent over, gasping, trembling all over, phone in hand. "They t-took Sam and Bryn," she panted.

Nev sucked in a breath. "*What?*"

Christa whirled, pointing as she brought her phone to her ear. "Over there. They—" She stopped and faced them again, her shoulders heaving. "Two of my friends were just kidnapped," she blurted out, Nev guessed to a 911 operator. "At the Fort Sumter Visitor's Center."

Headlights cut across the parking lot. Nev automatically grabbed Christa and Emily, ready to run.

"It's Luke and Rayne," Emily said, hurrying toward the SUV.

Ben and Rhys would be on their way here in the other vehicle.

Luke was behind the wheel. He stopped sharply in front of them and rolled down the window. Rayne was already climbing out of the passenger seat. "What's wrong?" Luke demanded.

"Someone just took Bryn and Sam," Emily said, then pointed in the direction Christa had come from. "Christa's called 911."

Luke jumped out and grabbed Christa by the shoulders. "Where are they?" he demanded.

"That way." She pointed behind her, shaking visibly now. "I-I think I knocked one guy out, on the path back there." She sucked in a breath, her phone still in her hand. "Two more guys dragged Sam and Bryn into an SUV. I don't know which direction they went in," she choked out.

"I'll find them. Are the cops on the way?"

"Yes."

Luke faced Nev, expression tense. "Call Rhys and tell him what happened. I'll call Ben." He gripped Emily's shoulder. "Stay with Rayne. All of you, stay with Rayne." Finally, he turned to his son. "Don't take them to the house. Find a secure location, stay there, and wait for me to contact you."

Without waiting for a response, he took off at a sprint in the direction Christa had indicated.

Rayne ran up to grab Christa in a hug just as Nev yanked her phone from her purse to dial Rhys. *Oh, God, Sam...* And Bryn.

"You okay?" Rayne asked, taking Christa's face in his hands.

She managed a nod. "I c-couldn't stop them," she whispered, tears spilling over.

Rayne hugged her to his chest with one arm and corralled his mother and Neveah with the other. "In the SUV. Quick."

Nev rushed for it, fingers shaking as she hit Rhys's code on her phone and clambered into the backseat of the waiting vehicle. Fear twisted inside her as Rayne jumped behind the wheel and took off, racing them away somewhere in the darkness.

The phone rang in Nev's ear. "Pick up," she whispered, her heart racing.

"Hey," Rhys answered, the hint of a smile in his deep voice. "How did the tour go?"

Nev swallowed back the tears gathering at the back of her throat, hating everything about this. Ben was going to be destroyed when he found out. "Someone just took Sam and Bryn."

Chapter Ten

Luke raced up the sidewalk, scanning for threats and any sign of the guy Christa had brought down. He didn't know how she'd done it, and didn't care, he was just glad she was safe. But to have any chance of saving Sam and Bryn, he had to find out where they'd been taken.

He caught a flash of movement in the shadows to his left, and veered toward it. A man was staggering to his feet, his back to Luke. Luke barreled toward him, seeing the blood on his face as the man stumbled around, his face illuminated by a streetlamp near the corner of the road.

Luke dove at him, catching him around the ribs in a flying tackle. They hit the ground with a thud, and Luke rolled fast. The guy grunted as Luke pinned him flat on his belly, catching the meaty wrists in his hands.

"Who are you working for?" he snapped, shoving the hands higher up toward the man's shoulder blades. This had to be about the letter and intel Sam had received. There was no other explanation.

"Get the fuck off me!"

Luke jammed his knee into the middle of the guys' spine, earning an enraged shout. "Who do you work for?"

The cops would be here soon to deal with this piece of shit. Luke planned to have what he needed and be gone by then. "Talk, or I start breaking bones."

"Joe Hanes," he growled out.

Fuck. "Where did they take the women?"

Idiot tried to struggle. Luke jammed his knee harder into the bastard's spine and laid a forearm across the side of his neck, applying his body weight behind it.

The guy choked and bucked beneath him, but Luke held fast, and only let up on the pressure after he'd gotten his point across. Blood poured down the guy's face from a wound in his forehead. Christa had hit him hard with something. Good for her.

"Where are the other women?" Luke snarled.

"The...fort," he rasped out, eyes bulging under the pressure of Luke's forearm.

Fort Sumter? "Why?" he pressed. He could hear the wail of sirens somewhere in the distance. Hopefully coming here.

"Wants...address," the guy wheezed.

"What address?"

"To the storage...unit."

Jesus. This was the first Luke had heard about it, but whatever was in that unit must be incredibly damning for Hanes to go this far to find it.

Luke had what he needed for now, and time was running short. He let up on his hold just long enough to haul back his arm and land a solid punch against the man's temple. The big body beneath him instantly went slack.

Luke got up, dragged the unconscious man to the sidewalk and dumped him in the circle of light beneath the nearest streetlamp, then took off running across the road as he pulled out his phone and dialed Dec's number.

He needed to find them a fast boat.

****

Dec's eyes snapped open when his cell phone rang. He rolled over and grabbed it from the bedside table, finding Luke's number on the screen.

"Yeah," he answered, his voice thick with sleep. He'd been deep under when that ringtone went off.

"Dec, listen to me."

He stilled, unease tightening his muscles. Luke's voice was uneven, as if he was running. What was going on?

"Joseph Hanes is here, and he just took Bryn and Sam."

"What the *fuck*?" Dec snapped, shooting to his feet, his heart thudding hard.

"He's taking them out to Fort Sumter."

Dec was already partway down the hallway heading for the stairs, his mind going a million miles an hour as he thought of Bryn and possible rescue scenarios. "Why?" he demanded. What the fuck did Hanes want with Bryn, or Sam?

"He wants an address to a storage facility. Has to be in what Sam was sent the other day."

Jesus. "Where is it?"

"In my study. Grab the piece of paper on my desk and the flash drive with Sam's laptop. Then go down into the basement and get enough weapons and gear for four of us, and meet me at the marina near Liberty Square next to the Fort Sumter Tour building, A-fucking-SAP. You copy? We can't afford to wait for the cops to respond to this. Every minute counts."

"Yeah, copy." Fuck!

He ended the call, shoved his phone into his jeans pocket and raced down the stairs, his muscles taut with a chaotic mixture of rage and panic. He battled to force all emotion from his mind as he ran into Luke's study and grabbed the piece of paper and flash drive from the desk.

But Jesus, Hanes had Bryn, and that traitorous son of a bitch had been working with Kader behind everyone's backs.

Running now, he found his way into the basement and flipped on the light to illuminate the small arsenal Luke had stored down here. He grabbed comms equipment, weapons and ammo, and started stuffing it all into a large duffel he'd found on a shelf, the seconds ticking loud in his head as they passed.

He thought of Bryn. Of how strong she was, and how terrified she must be right now in spite of that. She would fight. And with a man like Hanes, that put her in even more danger.

His heart hammered in his ears, his mind screaming at him to move faster. *Hold on, baby. I'm coming.*

Without pause, he whirled and raced back up the stairs and out of the house, running for his rental car. No matter what else happened tonight, he was going to save his wife.

****

"I still can't get over it," Ben said to his twin, shaking his head as they walked along the row of stores in the historic center of Charleston, past holiday shoppers out grabbing last-minute gifts. Like they were supposed to be.

Ben already had Sam's gifts, but he wanted to get something for Nev and the baby now, and Rhys needed to get her something special to mark their momentous news too. "That you're gonna be a dad."

"Yeah, I know."

No one else would be able to tell, but Ben knew his brother like he knew himself, and Rhys was secretly scared shitless. He found it freaking hilarious that Mr. Calm, Cool and Remote would be rattled about the prospect of becoming a parent. "Mom and Dad are gonna freak."

"Yeah." Rhys kept walking, glancing around at the shops they passed.

Ben loved his brother, but trying to have a conversation with his closed-up twin about meaningful shit was painful at the best of times. "You're excited though, right? I mean, aside from worrying about all the shit beyond your control?" It had been like pulling teeth, but Rhys had finally admitted he was worried something would happen to Nev and the baby between now and when it was born.

"Yeah."

Ben rolled his eyes and prayed for patience. Nev had gone a long way toward cracking through Rhys's remote outer shell, but his brother needed to drop the whole cyborg thing once and for all before the baby came along. "You thought about names yet?"

"Not really."

Course not. Couldn't let himself relax and actually start looking forward to something. In Rhys's mind, that meant it might get taken away. "Well, if you need any help, Ben's an awesome name for a boy. Or, maybe Benita or something for a girl."

Those dark blue eyes shot to him. "I can only handle one Ben at a time in my life," he said in a dry tone.

Wow, an attempt at a joke? Amazing. "I can't wait for the baby to get here. I'm gonna teach him or her all about the Red Sox, how to play catch, and some slick self-defense moves. Mostly I'm looking forward to filling your kid full of sugar when he or she comes for a sleepover, and then dropping them back off at your place right when the high kicks in."

"You would, too."

Absolutely.

"But payback's a bitch. I'll return the favor when it's your turn."

"I'm gonna be the favorite uncle." And Sam would

be an awesome aunt. She balanced him out with her serious nature.

"You're gonna be the *only* uncle," Rhys pointed out. "And how are you gonna have my kid over for sleepovers when you're in Virginia and we're in New York? You think I'm putting my kid on a plane every weekend to come see you?"

"Hey, who said it was gonna be every weekend? Okay, it'll probably be most weekends. And one of us is just gonna have to move, that's all."

Rhys looked at him in surprise as they walked along the cobbled street closed to traffic, open only to pedestrians. "You'd move just to be closer to my kid?"

"Yeah, of course," Ben said, wondering how his twin could think otherwise. "Though it would be easier for us if you guys moved south, since Sam and I are both still doing contract work in our area." Rhys was working behind the scenes as a consultant now, like Luke. "I dunno, I haven't talked to her about it yet, but I don't want to be the kind of uncle my niece or nephew only gets to see twice a year."

One side of Rhys's mouth kicked up in the hint of a grin. "Good to know."

Ben frowned. "Why, did you think I wouldn't want to be involved?"

"No, I just didn't realize you would be so into it."

Ben stopped walking to scowl at his brother, insulted. "You know, sometimes I wonder if I'm the only one of us that has the twin connection thing going. Because yours is either broken or missing entirely."

Rhys grinned and reached over to ruffle Ben's hair in a rare show of affection. And in public, too. "Whatever, punk. I've got it too."

"Yeah, and it sure shows," he grumbled, starting forward again. They'd passed a couple kid/baby stores but he hadn't seen anything in them that he liked. "I'm gonna get the baby a BoSox onesie and a hat, so don't order that yourself. Stick to camo or whatever."

"What if it's a girl?"

"Then get pink camo." Duh.

"Pink camo," Rhys muttered with a low chuckle, then went quiet as his cell rang. He pulled it out of his pocket just as Ben's rang.

Ben pulled his out. Recognizing the number, Ben answered. "Hey, Hutch. What's up?"

"Ben."

Ben stopped walking, dread curling in the pit of his stomach at Luke's tone. Five feet away, Rhys was talking rapidly to someone else, his body tense, face tight. "What?" he demanded, anxiety building at Luke's tone.

"Joe Hanes is here."

No...

"And he just took Sam and Bryn. They're heading for Fort Sumter."

It took a moment to process the words, everything around him funneling out except for the panic flooding him and the roar of blood in his ears. "What?" His voice was low, taut as fear crawled up his spine. *Sam...*

"Dec's on his way to the waterfront with weapons and gear. Meet us at the marina at Liberty Square in ten minutes, because we're going after them right now."

Chapter Eleven

"Let's go," Joe ordered, and threw open the SUV front passenger door just as the driver jerked to a halt in the marina parking lot several miles from where they'd taken the women.

Weapon in hand, he started for the wooden dock jutting out into the water. Two of his men were already at the fort, waiting for them. Another was guarding the Zodiac.

There was no one else around. He turned and waved two more of his men forward. They dragged the prisoners from the vehicle and hustled down the gangplank.

Both women were struggling in spite of the duct tape across their mouths and their hands secured behind them. The dark-haired one obviously had some training because she was putting up enough resistance to give Thomas—a former Green Beret—a hard time.

Joe hurried down the wooden dock to the Zodiac and jumped aboard. "Any trouble here?" he asked the man at the helm.

"Negative."

Good. Because they had only minutes to make their

getaway.

Taking the women in such a public place wouldn't have gone unnoticed, especially since one had gotten away and the last member of Joe's team hadn't responded to his calls. The cops would likely already be after them.

He swung around at the sound of running footsteps on the wood, and a low, muttered curse. The dark-haired woman had managed to get free of Thomas's grip and was trying to make a run for it, darting back up the dock.

Joe rushed for the stern of the boat, ready to race after her, but Thomas was already on her.

He tackled her, landing hard on the wooden planks, Thomas on top. The brunette must have had the air knocked out of her because she only struggled weakly this time when Thomas seized her and threw her over one shoulder.

Samarra was struggling too now, bucking in the other man's grip, and getting nowhere. Not surprising that a civilian tech contractor didn't have much if any hand-to-hand training, but Joe would keep a close eye on the brunette until they got to the fort.

His men hauled the women aboard the Zodiac. The instant the brunette was pulled in, Joe gave the signal and the helmsman fired up the engine. They pushed away from the dock and swung out into the dark, quiet marina.

"Hit it," Joe commanded. They couldn't afford to lose a moment.

The engine opened up with a throaty roar. The bow lifted, bouncing over the surface of the calm water as they sped out into the harbor. Joe's hair whipped around his face as he scanned the shoreline for any sign that the cops or someone else was following them, but saw nothing.

He turned to face the bow and the mouth of the harbor. Their destination lay ahead in the distance, a low-lit island fortress a mile or so out into the harbor.

It was closed now and all but deserted except for the

Park Rangers on duty. The security cameras were about to be temporarily offline, and it bought him some time in a secure place to interrogate his prisoner. Once there, he would hopefully get the intel he needed, and alert the remainder of the team standing by in the city. Now he needed to verify their exfil.

He pulled the radio from his hip and contacted the helo pilot waiting for his signal. "Start countdown now," he ordered.

Tucking the radio away, he turned to face his prisoners. Both women had stopped struggling. Thomas had the brunette at the far end of the stern. She glared at Joe with utter loathing.

Ignoring her, Joe stalked toward Samarra, the moonlight revealing the terror and fury on her face. No reason to wait now that they were away from shore. He could start the interrogation now.

Crouching in front of her, he ripped the tape off her mouth. She winced and jerked her head back, but he grabbed a handful of her hair and yanked her head to the side. "What did he send you in that envelope?"

Her jaw set, her eyes narrowing.

Joe jerked on her hair, his temper fraying. He was working on a short deadline and didn't have time to fuck around. "What was in that envelope, Samarra?"

Her throat worked as she swallowed, her face tight with discomfort from the angle he had her neck bent at. "Flash drive," she said.

He'd figured. And he also had a pretty good guess as to what was on it. Not that he could do anything about it if she'd already sent the files to someone else. "What else?" He needed the location on that goddamn storage unit. She had to have it. Had to.

Her mouth tightened and he wrenched her neck back even farther, until she grimaced, her body straining to alleviate the pressure on her neck. "Let go," she snarled.

Not on your life.

"Coming up on our approach," the helmsman yelled back to him over the wind.

Joe held Samarra's angry stare for a long moment, then released her hair with a shove and got to his feet. She thought she wouldn't talk, but she was wrong. He was an expert at extracting intel from reluctant prisoners.

He would have her blurting out every last secret she had before he killed her.

SAM STIFLED A cry as Hanes released her with a shove, sending her slamming back into the solid wall of the man holding her captive.

Hanes was crazy. To pull something like this here, he was desperate and insane.

And that made him incredibly unpredictable and dangerous.

Her mind whirled as the cold wind whipped over her face, the long strands of her hair lashing her skin and the haze of alcohol long since burned away. Bryn was aboard with her, but Christa might have gotten away. Maybe she'd called for help. If she had, she would tell Ben and Luke and the others what had happened. If she hadn't gotten away, then...

Then Sam and Bryn were on their own.

No, she told herself, refusing to give into despair. Christa must have gotten away, and called the others. Ben would know what had happened to her. He would come for her and Bryn with the other guys.

Sam stubbornly clung to that hope, and it was the only thing keeping the fear from turning into abject terror.

The boat bounced over the surface of the water. She squinted, looking past Hanes and the man driving the boat. A low, shadowy island sat ahead of them in the water, most likely Fort Sumter. They seemed to be heading straight for it.

As soon as the thought crossed her mind, the man driving the boat cut back on the engine. The bow dropped as the craft slowed. There was only minimal lighting at the fort, but enough for her to see a dock jutting out into the water, and that it appeared deserted.

The driver steered past the dock, however, heading around the back of the island before angling the bow sharply toward shore. The rubber hull scraped over rocks as the bow pulled up onto the beach.

Hanes leaped ashore, talking to someone on a handheld radio. Then he turned and gestured at the men in the boat. Sam's pulse tripped, then she stiffened when the guy holding her suddenly wrenched her upward by the arms. A cry of outrage and pain shot from her as her shoulder joints protested the painful jolt.

She struggled but was no match for the man's strength. He subdued her with demoralizing ease and dragged her from the boat onto the rocky shore. Her shoes slipped on the wet rocks. She stumbled, hit her knees on the jagged edges before he hauled her to her feet and forced her up the beach toward the fortified wall enclosing the fort.

Glancing back, she saw Bryn being propelled up the beach behind her. Sam's head snapped back when the man holding her shook her roughly.

"Move it," he snapped, his hand like an iron band around her upper arm, digging in with bruising force.

Her heart thudded painfully against her ribs as he pushed her toward the wall looming ahead in the darkness. Someone rolled a flexible ladder down the side of it.

Sam dug her feet in, her whole body rebelling at the sight of it and what it meant. She didn't want to go into the fort. Instinct warned her she would die in there if she did.

But the man holding her ignored her resistance, bent

and threw her over his shoulder then grasped the edges of the ladder. "If you don't want to fall and break your neck, hold still," he warned, and started climbing, one arm locked around the backs of her thighs.

Every muscle in her body went rigid, the fear intensifying as he carried her up the side of the wall while she hung over his back. Cold sweat broke out across her skin. What would happen once they were inside? Hanes might torture her. Torture Bryn, to make her talk.

Her whole body turned clammy, her breathing shallow. What did Hanes want from her? How could she drag this out and hold on long enough for help to reach them?

The world spun as they reached the top of the wall. Sam was unceremoniously handed off to someone else, dumped over another broad shoulder and then they were descending into the fort.

Hanes was waiting for her at the bottom. When the man holding her dumped her on the ground, Hanes seized her by the upper arm and hauled her to her feet.

Sam shot upward, her only option to obey if she didn't want her shoulder dislocated or her arm broken. She glanced past Hanes to take in their surroundings. Only a few lights were scattered around the dark interior, but it was enough for her to see they were behind what must be the visitor's center set in the center of the fort.

She scrambled to keep up with his long strides as he dragged her over to some old masonry work structure and shoved her down. Her ass hit the ground with a teeth-jarring thud. She quickly straightened, her back against the cold bricks as Hanes towered over her, a menacing wall of shadow in front of her.

He squatted down, the faint light filtering down from overhead making his eyes glitter menacingly. "What was on the flash drive?" he said in a low, deadly voice.

She swallowed, glanced to her right just as Bryn came into view, being herded toward them by her captor.

A hard hand grabbed Sam's chin and forced her head around. Hanes leaned in closer, his grip painful. "What was on it?" he repeated, face hard.

The man dragging Bryn thrust her down against another masonry structure about twenty feet away. Sam forced a steadying breath, trying to slow her racing mind and heart. She had to start talking, and there was no harm in telling him what was on the drive. "Numbers."

"What kind of numbers?"

The fear was trying to choke her, slowly closing her throat. "Bank accounts. Possible withdrawals and deposits. There were no names, no businesses."

His stare never wavered. "Did you make a copy? Send it to anyone?"

"No." Not yet. Though she'd planned to send everything to Jamie once she got the okay from Luke.

Hanes set his jaw, and her stomach tightened. He didn't believe her. She leaned back instinctively but there was nowhere to go. "What else did he send you?" he said.

She had to be careful. She had to give him enough information to make him believe she was cooperating and telling the truth, but not so quickly that any potential rescue attempt wouldn't get here in time.

Except she didn't know what the hell to do or say to delay any of this—or if help was even coming. "More numbers. Written on a piece of paper."

"An address?"

Stall. You have to stall. "I don't know. Maybe."

"Tell me the numbers."

What the hell was Hanes hiding that he would go to all this trouble to retrieve what Sam had been sent? "I didn't memorize them," she lied.

She'd absolutely memorized all the numbers from the start, but this was the only way she knew to delay what she feared was the inevitable. Once Hanes had what he needed from her, she was expendable. Which meant she was dead, and Bryn too.

"What else."

She hesitated a second, her mind working frantically and coming up with nothing helpful. "A key. I don't know what it's for. Who sent it?" Maybe if she could get him talking, she could buy a few minutes.

His expression hardened. "Doesn't matter. Do you still have everything?"

"I don't have anything now," she said, playing dumb and hoping he would buy it. "And your men destroyed my phone when they took me."

He released her jaw and eased back onto his haunches to stare at her. Sam held her breath, wondering what was going on in his head and whether she'd just earned her own death sentence. "Where is it?" he asked, his low voice sending a shiver up her spine.

Sam's heart thudded. She didn't want to tell him but she had no choice. She couldn't provoke him now, and just prayed what she was about to say wouldn't get any of the others killed. "At a house in Charleston."

"Luke Hutchinson's place."

Ice slid through her, even though she'd instinctively known he'd been aware that she was staying with Luke and Emily. He must have been watching her for a few days now if he'd found and taken her tonight.

He might even have been watching Luke's place the last couple days, and maybe everyone else's movements too. "Yes," she whispered, quaking inside. She was cold now. Cold to the marrow of her bones, desperately trying to think of a way to save her and Bryn.

"Where in the house?"

The quiet question made tears sting the backs of her eyes. Once she told him, Hanes's men would attack the house. People she loved would be hurt, and maybe even killed.

Hanes cocked his head, waiting.

"I can sh-show you," she said. "If you take me there, I'll show you."

Hanes's mouth twisted in a cruel smile. "Nice try, sweetheart, but no. You're gonna tell me exactly where it is, then I'm gonna send someone to get it."

Sam swallowed and opened her mouth to try and plead her case, but the words wouldn't come out.

She saw the moment Hanes's patience snapped.

His hand flashed downward. Sam tracked its movement, her heart seizing in horror when he drew a pistol, chambered a round and pointed it directly at Bryn.

Bryn's gaze shot to hers in terror, and Sam's stomach pitched. She wrenched her attention back to Hanes, fear and helplessness washing over her. No matter what she said now, someone she loved would die. "No, don't, *please*," she begged.

Hanes kept her pinned with that malevolent stare, his finger curved around the trigger. "You've got five seconds to tell me exactly where everything is, or she gets a bullet in the head."

Chapter Twelve

The chilly wind whipped over Ben as he leaned forward to balance his weight in the Zodiac. Rhys had the throttle wide open, racing them across the dark harbor toward the fort sitting on a low island ahead of them.

Sam was out there. He was desperate to get to her.

Luke and Dec were ahead and to the left in another boat. They would come in from the left side while Ben and Rhys would come in from the right.

Ben clenched his jaw, itching for the moment they reached the fort. How the fuck had this happened? He was terrified for Sam. She'd been through so much already—they all had—and now she and Bryn had been taken captive by an asshole CIA officer trying to cover his traitorous ass.

He tightened his grip on the rifle Dec had handed him and adjusted his NVGs. They were still dressed in their street clothes and had minimal gear, whatever Dec had been able to grab from Luke's loadout room in the basement. And in about another two minutes, they would be facing a series of potentially deadly unknowns.

They had no idea how many enemy fighters were

waiting for them at the fort, or how heavily armed they were. They had no idea where the enemy was positioned, and there'd been no time to coordinate much of a plan between them.

Salt spray washed over him as the Zodiac bounced over a small wave. Ben barely felt the cold, the fire in his gut burning hot. Sam's life was at stake. She was depending on him to pull her out before it was too late, and he wasn't going to let her down. He'd die first.

"Heading left," Luke said through Ben's earpiece. "See you on shore."

"Roger that," Ben responded. He tapped Rhys on the shoulder to signal him, his gaze fixed on the outline of the fort as it loomed closer. The dock and main entrance were no-gos. They had to assume that whoever was inside was guarding both, and might have lookouts or cameras posted for anyone approaching.

Fortunately, Luke knew the fort well from his time living in Charleston, and had told them about another way in.

If it worked, they might be able to maintain the element of surprise. If not, they would be walking into a kill zone. Didn't matter. Ben would either get Sam the hell out of there, or die trying. And there was no one else he would rather have with him right now than his twin.

Rhys cut the engine a ways out to conceal their approach. He and Ben grabbed paddles and pulled their way toward the right side of the island, staying out of the reach of the few lights to avoid detection. Through his NVGs he didn't see anyone standing at the top of the wall ringing the fort.

That didn't mean no one was watching, however. Hanes must have taken out whatever security was at the fort. The cops had been alerted to the situation but there was no time to lose, and they didn't have the training Ben and the others did.

At the last possible moment, they cut left and paddled hard for the shore. Sweat gathered along his spine, slicking his back, chest and face, his muscles straining to pull them to the beach.

They slipped into a spot on the rocks and leaped out, both of them breathing hard. There was no cover here, and no concealment. They had to move fast.

Weapon up to scan for threats, Ben raced for the shadows along the base of the wall, with Rhys right behind him. He pressed his back to the wall and peered to the left. The hidden entrance Luke had told them about was supposedly twenty yards or so away.

"In position," he murmured just loud enough for his mic to pick up.

"Copy," Luke responded. "We're moving toward the entrance now."

He began creeping forward, his left shoulder hugging the wall to make the most of the deep shadows. *Hold on, Sam. I'm coming.*

Even with his training and experience, he couldn't completely ignore the anxiety grinding in the pit of his stomach. They had no idea what they would find on the other side of this wall. There was no backup coming. They were all on their own, winging it and relying on experience and instinct while Sam's and Bryn's lives hung in the balance.

"Coming your way in two seconds," Dec murmured through the earpiece.

Right on cue, a big silhouette appeared around the far corner of the wall. Dec. Then Luke, a moment behind him.

Ben angled his weapon upward, keeping watch for anyone on the top of the wall as they converged on the entry point. He could hear Rhys behind him, their movements barely audible over the quiet lap of the water against the rocks below.

Ben lowered the muzzle of his weapon, directing it at the ground as he angled his body to approach the door. Dec did the same, mirroring his position as they converged on it together from either side, with Rhys and Luke keeping watch.

Ben's NVGs cast a green wash over everything, amplifying the minimal moonlight coming through the clouds. In the middle of the fortified wall, he found the iron door. Old, but the locking mechanism looked more modern.

Ben nodded at Dec, who pulled the high-powered torch from his pocket and began cutting through the lock. Ben checked all around them while the metal began to glow and hiss under the focused beam of heat.

Then he caught a flash of something out of the corner of his eye.

Instantly he raised his weapon, staring into the night sky where a small light was blinking. The outline of the aircraft slowly materialized, and the telltale sound of rotors vibrated through the air.

"Incoming," he murmured, his insides tightening. What now?

The helicopter was heading straight for the fort. Giving them only minutes to get inside and rescue Sam and Bryn.

****

Joe kept his weapon aimed directly at the brunette's head while he held Samarra's frightened gaze. Anger and impatience boiled inside him.

He reined them in with effort, ready to make good on his threat and pull the trigger just to prove his point. Did she think he was bluffing? That he wouldn't kill her friend to get what he needed?

"In the study," she blurted, her gaze shooting to the brunette and then back to him. "Please—"

"Where's the study?" he demanded, completely un-moved by her pleas. When he sent the remainder of his team to Hutchinson's house, they needed to know exactly where they were going. It had to be a quick, surgical in-and-out op. All Joe needed was the storage unit location.

"Main floor. Down the hall from the kitchen, closer to the back of the house. Now please, let us *go*."

Joe stared at her. He was good at reading people, yet all he was seeing from her now was fear and desperation. He couldn't tell whether she was telling the truth.

But he didn't have time to test it by making this ug-lier for her at the moment. His ride would be here momen-tarily, and the cops shortly thereafter.

He lowered the weapon, noting the way she sagged in relief as he pulled the radio from his hip. He would keep using the leverage of her friend's life against her. "The key and letter are in Hutchinson's study. Main floor, near the back of the house. Get them, text me a picture of what-ever's on that letter, and meet at the rendezvous point. Out."

As soon as he put the radio back, his burner phone buzzed. The pilot, signaling him that he was inbound.

Joe reached for Samarra. She shrank back, tried to scuttle away but he grabbed her upper arm and jerked her to her feet. "Let's go," he told Thomas, and stalked past him and the brunette.

"I told you what you wanted to know," Samarra pro-tested, yanking against his hold and trying to dig her feet in. "Let us *go*."

Nope. "I'm not done with you yet." Not by a long shot.

He'd find out soon enough whether she'd lied or not. If she had, he'd kill the brunette for starters. If that still wasn't enough to loosen Samarra's tongue, he'd start fill-ing her with holes until she gave him what he wanted.

He ignored her protests and her struggles and

dragged her along the back side of the visitor's center, past the ladder still dangling down the rear interior wall of the fort. She kept twisting, trying to break free.

Five seconds later his patience snapped.

He shoved her away from him, knocking her off balance so that she stumbled and fell onto her side. "You deal with her," he growled to another of his men, who hurried over to heft her over his shoulder. "And watch that one," he said to Thomas as he forced their other prisoner forward.

The brunette was trouble. Joe didn't trust her for a moment.

She was leverage, but in some ways it would be easier to put a bullet through her head and dump her here, save him the hassle of having to watch her. She seemed to know it too, because she didn't fight Thomas as he herded her along the back of the visitor's center.

Joe holstered his weapon and yanked the ladder down before leaving the old parade ground and heading around the far end of the visitor's center. On the other side of it was a clearing large enough for the helo to set down. Within moments of it landing, they'd be up and on their way to the RV point.

And as soon as he had the contents of that letter and confirmed the location of the storage facility, Samarra Sinclair would die.

He glanced up and to the right as the faint sound of rotors reached him. Stepping into the clearing on the other side of the visitor's center, he looked into the dark night sky and clearly saw the lights of the approaching helo. A private civilian aircraft he'd paid a shitload of money to rent, along with the pilot at the controls.

His men brought the prisoners around and stood waiting with him. *Come on, come on*, Joe urged impatiently.

It seemed to take forever. The helo slowly grew

larger as it neared them, the sound of the rotors getting louder. It slowed as it moved overhead, then gently descended into the clearing.

Joe seized Samarra's arm and began marching her forward just as its skids touched down, bending over a little against the force of the rotor wash. Just as his left foot touched the ground, concrete exploded in a burst where his head had been a second before.

He whirled and dropped to one knee, bringing Samarra in front of him. "Contact!"

His men instantly fanned out in a defensive perimeter. One jerked and went down, sprawled on his stomach.

Joe dragged his living shield closer, looking around frantically for the shooters but not seeing anyone. His men began to return fire.

Joe seized his chance, dragged Samarra upright and ran for the helo. Bullets cracked around them, the sound of the rifle fire echoing off the walls.

She tried to fight him, even angled her head to bite him. He cuffed her across the face and kept going, keeping her between him and the shooters.

The blast of the rotor wash intensified as they neared the aircraft. Joe seized the door handle, wrenched it open and climbed inside, keeping Samarra tight to him even as she kicked and bucked in his hold.

"Go, go!" he shouted at the shocked pilot, who nosed them forward and began to lift off the ground.

Heart pounding, Joe crushed Samarra to him. She was the currency he needed to escape. And in case his men on shore failed to retrieve what he needed, the only way to find what he needed to disappear and start over in Mexico.

Chapter Thirteen

Bryn jerked when the first shot echoed over the noise of the rotors. The man holding her grunted and dropped his weapon, his grip easing around her upper arm.

She tried to wrench free but he somehow managed to hold onto her despite being shot. More shots rang out from around her, the captors returning fire.

Her heart shot into her throat. *Dec.* It had to be Dec and Luke, come to save them.

She dropped to one knee, adrenaline and fear coursing through her in a dizzying rush.

Chaos reigned around her. She didn't know where Dec and the others were. Didn't know what she was supposed to do, or where she was supposed to go—but she wasn't going to just sit here and let someone grab her again.

She glanced to her left. Sam was already out in front of her, being dragged by a man toward the waiting helicopter. Bryn's heart sank, a sudden lump clogging her throat. There was nothing she could do for her friend.

The pressure around her arm let up even more as the guy leaned over to grab his fallen weapon.

A wave of anger tore through Bryn. They'd gagged her and bound her hands behind her, but she was still far from helpless. She had a fucking black belt, and Dec and Ben had shown her other handy tricks as well.

Sucking in a big breath of air through her nose, she whirled, bringing her right leg back and then snapping her foot forward with her full power behind it. The round-house caught the bastard in the back of the head just as he was straightening.

Pain radiated through the top of her foot and up her shin as he slumped forward. Bryn immediately adjusted her stance and lashed out again with her other foot, aiming for his face this time.

The blow never connected. He caught her shin and wrenched her leg upward, throwing her off balance. She twisted as she fell, hitting the ground on her shoulder. She rolled to one knee and pushed to her feet to bolt for cover as more shots echoed around her.

A foot caught her in the thigh, mid-step. She hissed in a pained breath as she went down again, rolling to her back just as her attacker lunged for her.

Bullets were still flying but she was too focused on getting free to worry about anything else. Baring her teeth beneath the gag, she reared both feet back and kicked out hard.

She nailed him in the chest, knocking him backward. Before he could recover, she leaped to her feet and stomped on the hand holding his rifle. He howled and shot out his other hand toward her, his face a mask of rage.

Bryn dodged it and spun to deliver a solid back kick, catching him in the side this time. He stumbled. She switched her stance, leaned her weight back on her rear foot, then slammed her dominant foot into the back of his skull. He collapsed.

Sucking in air through her nose, heart pounding so hard she felt sick, she kicked the fallen rifle out of his reach in case he regained his senses and took off across the courtyard as fast as she could. The shooting was behind her and to her right now, the reports echoing off the walls, mixing with the roar of the rotors.

She glanced over her shoulder to see the helicopter lifting, easing into the air as she tore across the open ground toward the shadows made by the far fort wall. She ran into a darkened bay formed by the interior brickwork and took a knee, panting, trembling as she took in everything before her.

She could see a few men lying on the ground, not moving, including the one she'd taken down. Others were moving around toward the shadows on the opposite side of the fort from her. She couldn't tell if they were friend or foe.

Dec, please be okay...

Wrenching her attention back to the helicopter, her heart sank as it rose into the night sky. Even if she and whoever was attacking the bad guys made it out of this alive, how were they going to save Sam?

****

She was trapped in a waking nightmare.

Sam's heart lurched as the helicopter lifted. The gunfire outside was intensifying. Muzzle flashes lit up the darkness below as the aircraft climbed into the air.

Hanes released her with a little shove that made her slump sideways, and scrambled to the far side of the open sliding door, a rifle in his hands as he scanned the ground. Sam's whole body trembled from a mixture of fear, shock and cold as the night air flowed in through the open door.

What was Hanes doing? Where was he taking her?

She couldn't see the people below them well enough to discern whether it was Ben and some of the other guys, but there was no way the police could have dispatched a tactical team this fast. She had to believe Ben had come for her.

She struggled to her knees, despair ripping through her as the helicopter cleared the wall of the fort. They were still low, still flying slowly. The water glistened below them in the moonlight, dark and deep.

She glanced at Hanes, who was still manning the door. He fired two rounds at someone below.

Rage punched through her that he might be shooting at Ben or one of the others.

He would kill her at some point. Whether when it was once he got clear, or when his men found the coordinates and key on Luke's desk. Right now, she was just his ticket to freedom, because he was banking that the rescue force below wouldn't try to take the helicopter down with her inside it.

The pilot began angling them higher.

Sam's gaze shot back to the water. It was a long drop already, and getting longer with every thudding heartbeat. But from where she was sitting, it was her only chance at surviving.

She looked back at Hanes. He still had his rifle to his shoulder, his attention on the ground.

Sam shifted her weight, easing forward even as terror flooded her. She didn't know how far up they were now.

Maybe the fall would kill her. With her hands bound behind her, maybe she'd drown. Maybe Hanes would shoot her before she made it out the door.

But jumping was the only way she could think of to save herself.

She glanced back at the fort, the lump in her throat all but choking her. If Ben was down there, she prayed he was okay. That he would make it out.

He would want her to do this. Would want her to do everything in her power to try and save herself.

I love you, Ben.

Tears blinding her, she reached down deep for all her courage, then lunged forward. Her shoulder barreled into Hanes, knocking him aside.

Then she was falling, her scream muffled by the gag as she plunged toward the inky water beneath her.

****

Ben tore back through the short tunnel that led to the exterior door they'd entered through, his heart in his throat. The guys were taking care of the remaining tangos inside. He was going after Sam.

The blood roared in his ears as he ran, his footsteps echoing off the concrete walls. He'd almost had a clear shot at Hanes when they'd first emerged through the door, then that fucker had pulled Sam in front of him and used her as a human shield so he could slink off to his helo, taking her with him.

Ben couldn't let him take her. Couldn't bear the thought of losing her, of living without her. All he could see was the look on her face as Hanes dragged her toward the helo. Terror and heartbreak.

I'm coming, sweet thing, hold on. Please hold on...

He burst out of the doorway and into the shadows on the other side of the wall. The helicopter had cleared the fort and was starting to ascend. He put his weapon to his shoulder, aiming at the open doorway. But he couldn't see Hanes.

A wave of sickening helplessness crashed over him. He couldn't take out the pilot without killing Sam in the ensuing crash. He was literally powerless. Literally unable to do anything to help Sam, even with all his skills.

A shattered scream of denial rose up his throat.

Movement from the helo doorway caught his attention. His muscles tightened. He sharpened his aim, finger on the trigger.

A figure flew out of the door. In the moonlight, he caught a flash of red hair.

His heart stopped. "*Sam!*" Her name tore from his chest in an animal roar of anguish.

He slung his weapon around his back and raced for the water, his legs like jelly. He saw the splash as she hit the water, then she went under and he lost sight of her. Someone inside the helo fired at her.

Ben reached back for his weapon, fury obliterating the fear. He took aim at the helo's open doorway, and the second he saw part of his target through it, he fired two shots in quick succession.

A figure toppled forward and fell into the water not far from where Sam had landed.

Sam. She had surfaced, but she was struggling, her head popping clear of the surface for a second, then going back under.

"Sam!" Ben dropped his weapon. She was eighty yards out or so. The water was cold and dark and she wasn't a strong swimmer.

He lunged for the edge of the rocks, his muscles bunching, ready to spring and launch him headfirst into the water.

"I got her!"

Ben jerked his head around just as Rhys flew past him and knifed into the water in a shallow dive. Ben raced after him, was steps from the water's edge when he heard the running footsteps behind him.

On instinct he turned, reaching for the rifle that was no longer there.

A man emerged from the doorway. Ben watched the muzzle of a weapon being turned toward him.

He reached for the pistol holstered on his hip just as the muzzle flash lit up the darkness. A bullet tore deep into his chest.

Ben jerked, his foot slipping, his right hand no longer

responding to his commands. The pistol fell to the rocks.

A bright burst of light, the sharp crack of a rifle. Another burning pain exploded through his ribcage.

He hit the ground, agony slicing through him. There was no air. He grabbed at his chest with his left hand, a terrifying, cold paralysis taking hold.

Two more shots rang through the darkness. If they hit him, he didn't feel it. And then all was strangely silent as he lay staring up at the moonlit sky, a strangled cry of anguish leaving his lips.

Sam...

****

Hanes had Sam on board the helo, and it had just cleared the fort wall, on its way back to shore somewhere. But the fight inside the fort wasn't over yet.

Dec stayed crouched behind the end of the visitor's center, scanning the battlefield in front of him. Luke was across the fort on the opposite end from him. Ben had just disappeared into the tunnel they'd entered from earlier, followed thirty seconds later by Rhys to track the helo.

Leaving Dec and Luke inside do deal with the surviving tangos. Dec liked those odds.

His gaze snagged on something moving to the right and snapped his head toward it, weapon to his shoulder and ready to fire. His NVGs caught a figure racing the last few yards across the old parade ground.

He sucked in a breath and removed his finger from the trigger. *Bryn.*

Only the discipline honed over a lifetime of service in the Teams kept him in place as he watched her run and duck behind cover, tracking her every move while guarding her six. A measure of relief slid through him when she was safely behind cover.

I'm here, baby. I'm coming for you.

120

As soon as he thought it, a tango emerged from around the end of the wall sixty yards in front of him. Dec waited. The man straightened and started sprinting toward where Bryn was hiding.

Dec squeezed the trigger, hitting his target in the neck. The man dropped where he stood, unmoving, his cervical spine severed.

He glanced toward Bryn's hiding spot. She peeked around the edge of the brick structure. *No*, he begged her silently. *Don't move.*

"Got a visual on Bryn," he murmured to Luke via his earpiece. "I'm going after her." They still didn't know how many tangos were left, but it didn't matter. He had to get to Bryn.

"Copy. I'll cover you."

Afraid she would bolt and expose herself to enemy fire if he waited any longer, Dec broke from his position, weapon up as he ran across the open parade ground.

A body emerged from behind another brick structure yards from Bryn. Dec swung the barrel of his weapon toward it and fired just as a shot ripped past him. More shots rang out behind him but he didn't stop, kept running, his sole focus on getting to Bryn so he could protect her and get her the hell out of here.

He was almost to the brick structure. A rifle shot cracked behind him, then silence.

Dec veered behind the bricks and skidded to his knees, stopping feet from Bryn. She sucked in a ragged breath and reared her foot back to drive it at his chest.

Anticipating the move, he leaned forward and caught her leg with both hands, taking away her leverage. "Bryn. It's me," he said in a low voice, flipping up his NVGs so she might be able to see him in the near darkness.

She cried out, sat up and threw herself at him. Dec caught her and held her tight to his chest. "Are you all right?" he demanded, running his hands over her, checking for injury.

She made a muffled sound and nodded, pressing closer. The bastards had bound her hands behind her and gagged her with duct tape.

He reached down, unsheathed his KA-BAR and sliced through the ties holding her wrists together. She grabbed hold of his shoulders, her eyes wide as she stared at him.

"Hold on. This is gonna sting," he warned, then grasped the edge of the tape and peeled it away from her mouth.

She winced, her fingers digging into his shoulders. "Hanes has Sam. He's got her in—"

"I know. Ben and Rhys have gone after her. Now come on. I'm getting you out of here." He bent to scoop her up in his arms.

"No," she protested, pushing at his chest. "I'm okay, I can run on my own. I'd rather you have your weapon ready."

He could easily use his weapon with her across his shoulders, but he trusted her to know her limits. "Stay right on my six."

"I will."

He crouched down behind the edge of the barrier, pulled down his NVGs and waited a few moments. It was quiet. Too quiet. "Bryn's okay. I'm bringing her out."

"Roger. No visual on any more targets currently. I'll cover you, then check the perimeter and meet you at the mouth of the tunnel."

"Copy." He turned to Bryn. "Ready?"

She nodded, the determination on her face making his heart swell with pride. His wife was a fucking badass.

Shoving to his feet, he picked a mental path back to the tunnel entrance and broke from cover. He could hear Bryn right behind him, his gaze scanning for any more threats standing between them and their only exit.

Another shot sliced through the quiet.

"Contact right, two o'clock, moving away from you," Luke said in his ear. "You got him?"

Dec couldn't see past the edge of the visitor's center yet. "Negative."

He stopped and pushed Bryn to her knees behind the corner of the wall, then brought his weapon up and ducked around the corner just in time to see a man reach the door to the tunnel. "Got him," he said to Luke, and broke from cover to pursue the final tango.

He had just entered the tunnel when he saw the tango at the other end raise his weapon to fire and race past the mouth out of view.

Shit.

Dec put on a burst of speed, emerging just as shots ripped through the air. He fired at the shooter, taking him out in a clean kill to the neck. But it was too late.

Ben was already lying motionless on the rocks.

Chapter Fourteen

The water was freezing, stabbing her like a thousand icy knives.

Sam flailed in the water, kicking hard, her restrained hands making it impossible to swim or keep her head above the surface. She managed to thrash enough to break through for an instant, dragging in a ragged, choked breath before she went back under.

Everything was cold and black.

Trapped beneath the surface, she craned her head back, eyes wide as she stared at the moonlight rippling across the surface above her. Miraculously she was still alive, had survived the jump and the fall and the bullets that had sliced through the water nearby. But she was tiring fast and she couldn't tell which direction the fort was.

Dimly she heard something hit the water close by. She kicked hard, propelling herself toward the surface, fighting with everything in her. She hadn't gone through all of this just to drown.

She had to get to shore. Ben might be there.

Her head broke through the water at last. She heaved in a breath of cool, sweet air, then rolled to her back, hoping to float.

A small wave washed over her head. She choked, panicked, her body automatically switching over to autopilot as her legs thrashed.

Something touched her calf. She almost screamed, barely remembered not to open her mouth as she kicked out.

Fingers clamped around her ankle, gripping tight.

Sam wrenched it free and struggled to the surface. She cleared it, coughing, managed to suck in a little more air before the hand grabbed her again.

Hanes. Still alive.

His other hand locked around her calf. Pulling her down with terrifying strength.

No! She lashed out with her other foot, her fingers curled into claws as she shoved them downward and raked them across the skin she met.

Hanes jerked and eased his grip. She lashed out with her heel this time, striking him hard.

The restraining hands fell away. Sam turned her face upward and kicked with all her might, terror flooding her as she broke the surface.

A sob ripped free, fear and desperation colliding. She couldn't see Hanes. Didn't know where he was, and she was still too far away from shore.

Please, someone help me!

This time she managed to roll to her back and keep her head above the water long enough to glance around at her surroundings. Overhead the helicopter was still climbing, flying away from her. She glanced behind her, managed to make out the shape of the fort, too far away.

She swam toward it, her movements jerky, expecting Hanes to grab her again at any moment. Her heart slammed against her ribs in a bruising rhythm, pounding in her ears.

Faster, Sam. Faster. She had to make it to shore.

Choking back another sob, she flattened out on her back once more and began kicking with all her might, hopefully heading toward the fort. Something splashed in the water nearby.

Her head snapped up, her heart careening in her chest. Someone popped through the surface twenty yards or so away. The moonlight caught on his face.

Hanes.

His head twisted toward her. Her heart stuttered as his gaze locked on her, then he slipped back under the water. He was coming after her again!

Sam immediately flattened out and kicked harder, desperate to get away from him, craning her neck every so often to make sure she was still heading toward the fort. Her limbs were already numb from the cold, her whole body shaking.

Fingers brushed the back of her thigh. She screamed and reared her leg back to slam her heel into Hanes. The solid contact vibrated up her leg, her skin crawling as she swam for her life, desperate to put distance between them.

Another agonizing minute passed. The cold was making it hard to breathe, sucking the precious air from her lungs. Her muscles were growing weaker with every second, her breaths coming in shallow little bursts as her body tried to warm her vital organs by shunting blood to her core.

She couldn't hear any shooting from the fort now, and the sound of the helicopter was fading, leaving nothing but the sound of the water splashing around her and the pounding of her heart in her ears.

She let out a sharp scream as strong hands grabbed her arms. *Hanes.*

"I've got you, Sam."

She froze, blinking at the sound of that wonderful, familiar voice. "Rhys," she gasped out, going limp with relief.

"I've got you. I need you to relax and let me tow you in."

"B-Ben," she said through chattering teeth, trying to

turn toward him.

His arm banded around her ribs like steel. "No, float on your back for me and let your muscles relax. I'll have you to shore in no time."

He hadn't answered her about Ben. It was impossible to relax, she was shuddering all over from the cold and shock, but she tried to do as he said.

Ben. If Rhys was here, then Ben was too. She would see him in only a few more minutes. She closed her eyes, pressed her lips together as tears of relief gathered.

Her eyes sprang open, her muscles tightening as she remembered. "Hanes," she rasped out. "He's—"

"Dead. I saw his body surface. He's gone."

What? She looked up into Rhys's hard face as he swam her to shore, and another thought struck her. *Bryn.*

She opened her mouth to ask about her friend, but he shifted his grip and angled her upward a bit. "Okay, almost there. You're doing great."

Less than a minute later he touched bottom. He pulled her with him, then lifted her into his arms as he began climbing up the rocks and out of the water.

She gasped when the cold air hit her wet body, moaned as the shudders got worse. "B-Ben," she managed.

"Ben!" he yelled as he pulled her free and began carrying her up the sloping shore. "Ben, I've got her!"

Sam was shaking so hard she could barely see. She blinked as Dec materialized out of the darkness with Bryn. Sam gave a glad cry to see that her friend was okay, her hands free and the gag gone.

"Where's Ben?" Rhys demanded.

Dec's face was somber in the moonlight as he stared at them. "He's hit."

All the air rushed from Sam's lungs. Her heart stopped beating.

Rhys went rigid against her. "What?"

Dec turned, his gaze moving up the shore. And then Sam saw them.

Luke was crouched over someone lying on his back on the rocks.

"*Ben*," she screamed, arcing upwards in Rhys's arms. She had to get to him. Had to help him.

Rhys clamped her to him and raced for his brother.

Pain unlike anything Sam had ever known engulfed her as Rhys finally reached him and set her down. "Ben," she quavered, dropping to her knees beside his head.

He'd been shot through the chest and side. His shirt was soaked in blood. His eyes fluttered open at the sound of her voice, slowly focused on her.

Luke was behind her, quickly cutting her wrists free. As soon as they were, she grabbed Ben's face in her hands. "Look at me," she told him. "Look right at me. I'm okay, and you're going to be okay too." Slowly those pale green eyes focused on her. "Hi," she whispered, her voice shredding.

His lips parted as if he was trying to talk. Then he choked, a trickle of blood spilling from the corner of his mouth.

Horrified, Sam swallowed a cry as Luke and Rhys immediately turned him onto his side. The sound of Ben's breathing was awful. A rattling, gurgling wheeze. The scent of his blood mixed with the salty air, making her stomach twist.

Rhys and Luke were talking, their words clipped, commanding, but she didn't hear a thing they said, and didn't even know who they were talking to, her or Ben. All she could focus on was her husband as she cradled his pale face in her icy hands.

"I'm here," she whispered helplessly as tears tracked down her face. "I'm right here, sweetheart, can you hear me?"

Ben struggled to suck in another horrible breath, and

closed his eyes.

"No. Ben, no, look at me," she pleaded.

The sound of a boat motor cut through the terrible silence. She glanced up, her vision blurred by tears as Dec steered a boat up on shore yards away from them. Bryn was in it with him.

Luke and Rhys immediately lifted Ben and rushed for the boat. Sam staggered to her feet and stumbled after them. Her teeth chattered, her heart fractured into a thousand jagged pieces that sliced her up with every shallow breath.

Ben had come here to save her. And now he was dying.

She knew he was. She could feel it. And the agony of it was too much to bear.

Luke and Rhys got Ben into the boat. Sam made it to the bow on her own, her mind whirling in anguish and shock, a scream of pain trapped in her chest.

Bryn was there, gripping her hand and helping her aboard. Sam jerked forward as Dec started the engine and immediately headed for shore.

She stumbled her way over to Ben, who was lying on the floor near the stern. She dropped to her knees beside him and clutched his hand, the weight of her grief crushing her. She couldn't take this. Not Ben. Never Ben.

She barely registered the sensation of warmth as Bryn wrapped her arms around her and held on tight. Rhys was pressing two wadded-up shirts to the wounds in Ben's chest and side, his face grim, eyes haunted as he laid a thin piece of plastic across the wound over Ben's lung to try and seal it.

Sam was vaguely aware of Luke on his phone, calling for help, asking for emergency medical transport to be standing by when they reached the marina.

Shaking all over, Sam clutched Ben's hand in hers and stared into his motionless face, willing him to hold on. To fight. For her. For *them*.

His eyes were closed. She couldn't even tell if he could hear her anymore.

Dissolving into tears, she bent low over him, putting her cheek to his. "Please, Ben. Please don't leave me," she choked out.

It was Christmastime. And Sam needed a miracle.

****

The pain was so intense he couldn't breathe.

Ben clung to the tenuous thread of consciousness, instinctively sensing that if he let go, he was done for. He faded in and out of consciousness, between blessed blackness and stark terror when the fear kicked in again, propelling him back to the surface, through the heavy, gray layers weighing him down.

Then the pain hit again.

His mind suddenly snapped back into gear. *No air.*

He tried to suck in a breath. Couldn't. His body arced, struggled in vain as panic punched through him.

Strong hands held him down. Voices floated around him.

His body settled, the pain and panic fading a bit as he slid back under. But somehow, he stopped it from taking him this time.

Beneath the pain and fear he could feel the cold wind whipping over him. He thought he might be shaking. And he could hear more voices around him now. Indistinct at first, then clearer as the pain sharpened and he eased back toward consciousness again.

"Ben. *Please*, Ben, you have to hold on for me. You *have* to."

Sam. Sam was talking to him. She was upset. Crying.

He vaguely registered the pressure around his hand. On his cheek.

Sam. He tried to squeeze her fingers in reply, but his hand wouldn't move. Nothing would move, not even his lungs.

He forced his eyelids open a fraction, fighting for every ounce of air, but it felt like they had lead weights attached to them.

Sam sobbed and leaned over him, her blurry face coming into view for a second. Her wet hair blew around her, spraying cold droplets on his face. She was pale. Terrified, her eyes filled with tears.

He hated that she was afraid and hurting. *Don't cry*, he tried to tell her, but his lips wouldn't move.

Then he became aware of the movement. They were on a boat. It was skipping over the water. And Sam was scared because he'd been shot.

"That's right, you hold on," she told him with a forced smile, staring into his eyes. "I love you so much. I know it hurts, but you have to fight. You're a fighter, Ben."

With herculean effort he shoved back the agony and fear bombarding him. He *was* a fighter. Had been since the day he was born. He would fight for her. Would do anything for her, and wished he could comfort her now.

"Ben. You listen to me," a hard voice said.

His gaze flicked over to see his brother hovering over him. Rhys was naked from the waist up, the muscles in his massive arms standing out as he applied pressure to the wounds in Ben's chest. Making them burn like hellfire.

His mind cleared a little more, the pain and adrenaline wiping away the shock.

Ben was a medic. He knew what the wound placement and symptoms meant. Both his lungs had collapsed, that's why he couldn't breathe. And he'd been shot in the side as well, possibly in the gut or liver. He must have lost a lot of blood.

"Don't you let go," Rhys growled, his eyes more intense than Ben had ever seen them.

Not going anywhere, Ben wanted to say.

Rhys's face was taut, all his focus on him. "Don't you fucking let go, you hear me, punk?"

And then Ben knew.

Holy fuck, I'm dying.

The pain suddenly increased tenfold. He tried to drag in a shallow breath, but there was no air.

None. Only pain, more than he could bear. It felt like someone had set his whole chest on fire, and had parked an elephant on it for shits and giggles.

Terror and grief ripped through him like a blast wave. He was fading fast. Could feel the blood pumping out of him, his strength ebbing, the cold increasing.

He stared up at his brother, tears rushing to his eyes. *No. Don't wanna die. Don't let me die.*

"Ben."

He shifted his gaze to his wife. She stroked his cheek, tears rolling down her face. "I love you," she whispered, as if she knew.

I love you. I love you, he wanted to scream. He wanted to hold on, he was fighting so hard to, but his strength was fading. The darkness was too powerful, pulling him down. Sucking him into the abyss.

With all his remaining strength, he tried to squeeze her hand. He thought his fingers moved a little.

He couldn't speak so he sent up a silent prayer to his brother, hoping his twin would hear it. *You take care of her for me.*

****

Nev snatched her cell phone from the table in the safehouse kitchen when it rang. Rayne and Emily were staring at her as she checked the screen. "It's Luke. Hello?" she answered.

"Where are y'all?" he demanded, his voice urgent.

Her spine jerked ramrod straight in the chair. "In a house across town. What's happened? Is Sam—"

"Sam and Bryn are both okay. But Ben's not."

Oh, Jesus. "What's wrong?"

"Shot twice in the torso."

No. She closed her eyes, her heart going out to him, Sam and Rhys. "How bad?"

"Bad. We're almost to shore and there's an ambulance standing by, but his vitals are dropping fast. Can you meet us at the hospital Emergency entrance? He's gonna need to go straight into surgery."

"Of course." She was already up and heading for the door, her mind spinning with a million questions.

"Rayne will take you, and Em knows the staff there. She can help get you into the O.R."

"Okay. I'm on my way. Tell Rhys I'm coming."

"I will."

She stopped and turned to tell the others, but Rayne and Em were already standing behind her. "We need to get to the hospital, *now*." She filled them in as she grabbed her purse and shoes. A minute later they were all piling into the SUV and Rayne raced them to the hospital.

They beat the ambulance there. Nev rushed inside with Em while Rayne stayed close to guard them, just in case. "Come on, I'll take you straight to the ER doc," Em said.

She took Neveah straight to the emergency physician and explained the situation. His answer wasn't good.

"The trauma and vascular surgeons are already busy performing surgeries right now. All we've got left is an on-call general surgeon. They've already called her in, but it'll be at least another fifteen minutes before she can get here."

That was too long, but what choice did they have? "I'll scrub in now and assist her." The surgeon would need a hand, and even though Neveah's weren't what they once were, they were better than nothing and Ben needed all the help he could get.

The ER doc shook his head and both she and Emily began arguing with him at the same time.

Nev's patience snapped five seconds in.

"I'm a certified trauma surgeon, and I need to scrub in now if we're going to have any chance of saving the patient's life," she snapped, cutting off the rest of what Emily was going to say. "So go call whoever you need to, but I'm going to be ready and waiting in that O.R. when the patient arrives."

The man's mouth tightened. He stared at her for a long moment, then nodded, no doubt only because of the circumstances and Em vouching for her. "Okay. Fine. Scrub in and I'll call the other surgeon."

Nev spun away and hurried with Emily to get ready. Her heart pounded as she put on a pair of scrubs and began her scrub-in procedure, the ritual so familiar and yet terrifying now.

She was about to operate on Ben to try and save his life with reduced sensation and motor function from the median nerve damage in her dominant hand. She scrubbed at her skin, feeling nothing along her right thenar eminence, or all the way up her thumb and index finger.

Anxiety clawed at her. She forced it aside and focused on what she had to do.

Someone tapped on the glass of the scrub room. She glanced up, and her heart constricted to see Rhys standing on the other side.

His face was strained, his shirt smeared with blood. And his eyes... The haunted, desolate look in them made her want to cry.

She lifted a hand, wishing she could go to him. Comfort him somehow. Reassure him that she would do everything in her power to save Ben.

He swallowed. Nodded.

Pain sliced through her when she caught the sheen of tears in his eyes as he turned away. The strongest man she knew, the one who hated showing any kind of weakness, crying for his twin.

Shaken, Nev turned back to the sink and began washing her arms, keeping her hands higher at all times so as not to contaminate them with any bacteria-laden soap and water.

The scrub room door opened and a bronze-skinned woman around the same age as her rushed in. "You Doctor Sinclair?" she asked, quickly removing her watch and wedding band.

"Yes."

"Sarah Chambers. Nice to meet you," she said, coming to the sink to start her own scrub-in procedure. "The patient's your brother-in-law?"

"Yes. Is the ambulance here yet?"

"Just got here as I was pulling in."

The operating room doors burst open on the other side of the large window in front of them. Neveah sucked in a breath as the team wheeled Ben in. His face was ashen beneath the oxygen mask. Blood soaked his torso and the gurney, dripping onto the linoleum floor.

She swallowed and pushed aside her fear, calling on her professional demeanor and training. "I'll see you in there."

Holding her hands up so they were higher than her elbows, she walked through the connecting door into the operating theater, praying that together they could save Ben's life.

Chapter Fifteen

Ben still hadn't regained consciousness.

Rhys sat up and leaned back in the chair he'd pulled beside his brother's hospital bed, stretching his stiff neck. He wasn't even sure what day it was anymore. How long had he been here? Three days now?

The room was eerily silent, the soft beeps and whirs of various equipment providing a rhythmic backdrop he hated with every fiber of his being, reminding him of his hellish recovery from the brain injury that should have killed him.

Now the tables had turned, and it was Ben fighting for his life.

His brother had required multiple transfusions to stop him from bleeding out. The surgery itself had taken forever. One bullet had perforated both lungs. Another had hit his liver.

Nev and the rest of the surgical team had stopped the internal bleeding and patched up the holes, but Ben was still in danger from internal hemorrhage and infection. They'd put him in a medically-assisted coma to keep him under and give his body a chance to start healing.

Now he had a fever due to an infection. They were

giving him strong antibiotics for it, but there was no guarantee he would pull through.

Rhys turned when the door opened behind him. Nev walked in and gave him a soft smile, looking tired. Here in the ICU the visitation rules were strict, only one close relative at a time. But since Nev was a surgeon and had operated on Ben, they'd allowed her in too.

"Hey. How you holding up?" she asked him quietly.

"Fine."

"Yeah?" She came over to the bed, paused to check the equipment and Ben's vitals, then slid into Rhys's lap and wound her arms around his neck. "You don't look fine to me," she murmured, their faces close together.

He drew a deep breath and let it out slowly. It was almost Christmas. They should all be celebrating the holidays together at Luke's place right now. Not sitting here praying his twin wouldn't die. "Have they said anything else? About when he'll wake up?"

"They've already reduced his meds, so he could wake up any time. Now it's just wait and see."

Rhys nodded once, his gaze straying back to his twin. The doctors had been tight-lipped about Ben's prognosis. Even Nev, not wanting to give him false hope.

This was total role reversal. Not so long ago it had been Ben sitting at his bedside, waiting, wondering if he would ever wake up.

Rhys had kept that same vigil ever since Ben had come out of surgery the other night. Because he couldn't leave his brother's side. Wouldn't.

"How's Sam?" he asked, because he needed to think about something else before he lost it. They'd had to force her to leave the hospital earlier, to go back to the safehouse and get some rest.

Between the shock of it all, then interviews by the Feds and cops about what had happened, and worrying herself sick over Ben, she'd been ready to drop. Rhys had sworn to her he wouldn't leave Ben's side, and that's the only reason she'd finally agreed to leave to have a shower and get some sleep.

"Distraught," Nev answered. "But we made the right call in making her go to the safehouse with the others. She's got Christa and Emily there to take care of her, and Dec and Rayne are on guard, just in case. She was still in shock and needed to sleep." She stroked the back of his hair. "And so do you."

He shook his head. "I'm fine."

He'd sat in the waiting room with his arm around Sam the entire time Ben was in surgery. She'd been checked, treated for mild hypothermia, then released, and gone straight to the waiting room, refusing to budge until she saw Ben. Luke had stood guard near the hospital entrance, watching for any sign of a threat in case some of Hanes's team were still out there.

"Where's Luke?" he asked.

"More meetings with Feds and Agency people."

He grunted. The cops had arrested a guy trying to break into Luke and Emily's house. There'd been a brief shootout and the perp was dead. One of Hanes's men, going after the letter and key Sam had received. But at least the last threat to them all was gone.

He could feel Nev's gaze on him, but he wasn't budging on this. When he'd suffered his traumatic brain injury, Ben hadn't left his side. Ever.

Little punk had stayed next to him, talking to him, riding his ass, coaxing and pleading and whatever else he'd said during those long days and nights before Rhys had regained consciousness. When Rhys had finally opened his swollen eyes, Ben's face was the first thing he'd seen.

Rhys could do no less for his twin now.

He cleared his throat, removing the lump sitting there. "How're Mom and Dad?" They'd flown in first thing the morning after the surgery and sat with Ben for a bit after Sam had seen him, one at a time, while Rhys stood just outside the door.

"Worried sick. I finally managed to convince your dad to take your mom to the hotel about ten minutes ago. I promised I'd call them the moment I got an update."

"That's good." He linked a hand with hers, loving her more than ever. The only thing that had stopped him from puking his guts out from raw fear when they'd whisked Ben into the operating room the other night was that Nev had been part of the trauma team.

He'd never be able to repay her for what she'd done. Or explain what she meant to him.

"I'll stay with him," Nev murmured, her voice soft, soothing. "He won't be alone."

"I'm not leaving." He set his jaw, his emotions all jumbled up as he stared at his brother's pale face. He thought about the smart-mouthed punk with the chip on his shoulder who'd been such a pain in the ass over the years—and also Rhys's best friend.

He swallowed, rubbed his fingers over his eyes as they began to sting. Imagining a life without his twin was unthinkable.

Nev stopped stroking his hair and got up, instinctively sensing his struggle and need for space. He hated coming unglued, but especially in front of anyone, and he was teetering on the verge of his control right now.

"Can't leave him," he rasped out, hoping she would understand. He wasn't pushing her away so much as he was desperately struggling to hold onto the last of his control.

She carefully eased a hip onto the edge of Ben's bed, watching him for a long moment. "If I go get you something, will you eat it at least?"

He dipped his head. "All right."

She bent forward, putting her hand on his cheek as

she leaned in to kiss him. "I love you and I'm here for you. Just don't forget that," she murmured, then got up to leave.

Rhys caught her wrist as she stepped past him, waited for her to look down at him before speaking. "I love you too," he said.

It seemed like a totally inadequate thing to say. She was his wife, the mother of his unborn child, and she'd helped save both him and Ben. He owed her far more than he could ever give in return.

Her smile was understanding, a little sad. "I know. I love him too. I just hate seeing you hurt."

Rhys didn't answer, just squeezed her hand in acknowledgment.

"Just talk to him. There's a chance he might be able to hear you," she murmured.

When the door slid shut behind her, leaving him alone, his grip on his control slipped another notch. He leaned forward in the chair and reached for Ben's limp hand, gripping it tight as he pulled in deep, slow breaths that became increasingly shaky.

He never cried, but he'd lost it in front of Ben last year when Nev had undergone emergency surgery to repair her severed artery and nerve in her arm. If he lost it now, no one would know. But shit it was hard, that ingrained need to keep everything locked down still as strong as ever.

Ben's pulse was steady on the monitor, his chest rising and falling with each breath. Rhys just wanted him to wake up. For Ben to open his eyes and say something irritating.

Holding his brother's hand, Rhys forced aside his discomfort and started talking. Anything he could think of that might make Ben fight harder.

"Sam's coming back soon," he told him. "We made her leave so she could get some sleep, but I know she'll be back here within a few hours. She's worried sick about you, punk. We all are."

He drew in a slow breath, feeling stupid at first for babbling, but soon he couldn't stop. "I can't wait to see you with the baby. You'll have to show me the ropes. And Mom and Dad are here too. They're beside themselves."

He paused, thinking of something else to say, and settled on a memory that stuck out. "Remember that Corvette we stole from the rich neighborhood that day? I couldn't figure out how to shift it into second and drove it straight into a fence."

He smiled, a bittersweet pang hitting him as he remembered it. "You hauled me out through the passenger door and helped me over the fence before the owner could catch us. Or when we broke into that Italian joint because it smelled so damn good and we hadn't eaten in over a day?"

Ben didn't move. Didn't react in any way, only the sound of the beeping filling the silence.

Rhys shook his head, feeling the grip on his control beginning to loosen. "We've always been there for each other. You can't leave me now," he finished in a ragged voice.

By the time Nev returned a while later with a tray of food for him, his throat was sore from holding back the tears gathering there. Again, she offered to stay, but he refused.

"You should go to the rental house and sleep for a while. Luke'll take you. I don't want you wearing yourself out." They were right on the cusp of the second trimester, but he still worried about her and the baby.

She sighed but thankfully didn't argue. "Then you get some sleep too. I'll call you in a while." She kissed him and left.

The fatigue weighed on him as he sat there in the quiet room. After another nurse came in to adjust something in Ben's line, exhaustion hit Rhys hard. He wound his fingers around Ben's hand, afraid to cut that connection between them. Afraid that Ben would let go and slip away if he did.

"You gotta fight harder, punk," Rhys told him, his voice rough. "You're gonna be an uncle in a few months. You... You can't make me do this on my own." His voice cracked. He squeezed his eyes shut, clenching his jaw as the grief pummeled him.

Through his struggle to battle the tears, the pattern of the beeping in the room changed. Rhys opened his eyes, his gaze shooting to the monitor showing Ben's vitals. His brother's pulse was picking up.

He reached for the call button to summon the nurse, then froze at the slight pressure around his fingers. His eyes shot to Ben's hand, then up to his brother's face. Ben's eyelids were flickering.

Rhys sucked in a breath and squeezed Ben's hand harder. *Oh, Christ, please...* "Ben. Can you hear me?"

A second later, Ben's fingers tightened weakly. Rhys exhaled and shut his eyes, tears welling up. He blinked and focused on his brother's face, his chest about to explode. "Fuck, yes. Come on back, Ben."

Ben's eyelids fluttered again. Cracked open a fraction, those pale green eyes focusing blearily on Rhys. He frowned. His lips moved.

"What's that?" Rhys leaned down close to Ben's lips.

"Look...like...shit," Ben whispered.

Rhys barked out a startled laugh, but it blew apart the door holding his emotions in check. He dissolved into tears, unable to fight them a second longer. He covered his face with one hand, his shoulders shaking.

A long-suffering sigh reached him, then there was a weak tug on his hand. "Hard ass." Another tug, this one a little stronger.

Rhys leaned over his brother, shoving his wet face into the side of Ben's neck while his chest split apart and the tears fought free.

Ben reached up to pat Rhys's back weakly. "There ya go," he rasped out weakly.

It poured out of him. Relief. Gratitude. Fear. Knowing how close he'd come to losing his other half. "You s-son of a bitch," he gasped out when he could finally breathe again. "You al-almost died on me."

"Did I? Sorry." Another weak pat on the back.

Rhys sat up and scrubbed at his face, sucking in a steadying breath. Shit.

"Where's Sam?" Ben rasped out.

He dragged his shoulder across his eye, mopping up the tears with his T-shirt. "We sent her to get some sleep. I'll call her right now." He dug out his phone, punched in Sam's number, but stopped when Ben put a hand on his.

His brother's eyes were hazy with a combination of pain and meds. "Thanks for staying."

Aww, shit. "I'll always be here for you," he vowed, and stood up to call Sam.

****

Everything hurt. Even his hair. But as much as the pain sucked, it meant he was alive, so it was worth it when Sam finally came through the door of his hospital room.

Seeing him, her big brown eyes immediately flooded with tears. She let out a sob and flew at him as Rhys finally stood and relinquished his post.

Ben closed his eyes as her arms wound around his neck. He reached up one hand, wincing as the motion pulled at the incisions in his chest and side, and stroked her back. She buried her face in his neck, her shoulders shaking with silent sobs, the scent of her shampoo filling his nose.

"Hey," he murmured, his own throat tightening. "I'm okay, sweet thing."

She only cried harder, clinging to him. He kept holding her as best he could, vaguely aware of his twin silently slipping from the room to give them privacy.

Everything about this was surreal. He'd thought for sure he was a goner during the boat ride from the fort. Didn't remember anything after going under that last time. But Nev and the rest of the trauma team had saved him.

And Ben had never been so grateful to be alive.

Sam finally calmed enough to lift her head. She wiped distractedly at her face, her tear-drenched eyes locked on him. "Oh, God, I'm so g-glad you're back," she whispered, gently stroking the side of his face with her free hand. "Are you in a lot of pain?"

"Not too bad. The nurses upped my meds before you got here, so it's better." But he'd bear any amount of pain to stay with her.

She blew out a breath and sat in the chair Rhys had vacated, looking exhausted. "Did Rhys tell you what happened?"

"Yeah." Hanes was dead, the fucker, along with most of his crew. The cops had shot one guy trying to break into Luke's place, and the only one of Hanes's men to survive had been the one Christa had taken down. The Feds were doing their thing with him now. "He said Christa took one guy out with a branch for a bat, and then hurled a rock into his face." It was just so awesome.

"Wish I'd been able to do that." She huffed out a breath. "I panicked when Hanes grabbed me."

"Hey." He reached for her hand, squeezed it. "You survived. You knew jumping out of that helo was the only way to save yourself, and you did it." He'd aged fifty years in those few seconds, watching her plummet into the water.

She shook her head. "I should never have brought that shit with me here. I should've left it at home or called someone to—"

"No one could've known what would happen. Not even you, as smart as you are." And she was brilliant.

Her eyes were haunted. "I'm so sorry this happened."

Ben shook his head, refusing to let her blame herself for any of this. "It's not your fault. Come here." He held out an arm gingerly.

She leaned back down and nestled her face into his neck again, her fingers running through his hair. "I love you so much. And I'm so glad you're still here."

"Love you too. And I'm not going anywhere." He was looking at a slow and potentially long recovery, but that was okay compared to the alternative. He had Sam, Rhys and the rest of his family to help him through it.

"Your parents are downstairs, by the way. They're dying to come up, but these ICU nurses are savage about enforcing the rules."

"In a bit. Just want you right now."

She kissed his cheek. "You've got me for always."

Ben closed his eyes, savoring the feel of her tucked in close to him. He'd needed a Christmas miracle, and somehow, he'd gotten one.

Chapter Sixteen

"Oh, it's good to be home again."

Luke glanced at Emily as he shut and locked the back door behind them. "Sure is."

It was December twenty-third. Four days since the night Hanes took Sam and Bryn. Luke hadn't let anyone come back here until the cops, Feds and the CIA could all confirm the threat was truly over, and not just because they'd recovered Hanes's body from the harbor the morning after the attack on the fort.

Dealing with all the fallout in between had been exhausting. Interviews and meetings. Then more interviews and meetings. They'd all been questioned separately, and Luke had gone out to Fort Sumter with the investigators to explain exactly what had happened. Now it was all done, and they could all try to get back to some semblance of normal.

He and Rayne had gone over every inch of the house earlier, checking for anything suspicious, but everything was as they'd left it. Hanes's guys hadn't made it into the house. Now he and the others were all dead, except for one, and that lone survivor had spilled everything during interrogation.

It was late, but at least now everyone was finally back under their roof again, except for Ben, who was staying in the hospital for another day or two, and Sam, who refused to leave without him.

He released the handle of Em's suitcase and put a hand on her lower back to nudge her toward the stairs. "Go on up and take a bath. I'll be up in a few minutes."

She glanced at him, the shadows beneath her eyes more prominent than ever. These last few days had added way too much stress to all of them, and he was sorry for it.

Thankfully Ben had pulled through, but it had been way too goddamn close. Luke was sick to death of the people he loved being in danger. And worse, this had happened in his city, on his watch.

"All right," she said, and moved past him to start up the curving stairs.

Luke strode straight to his study and slid the door shut. The note, key and flash drive were still on his desk. He'd sent all the intel to Jamie, his former boss and the only person he trusted in the Agency.

Jamie had come back with the news that Kader was dead, but not from a drone strike. Hanes had tortured and killed him in an abandoned Agency holding facility near D.C. the day Sam and Ben had flown down to Charleston. The Feds had found Kader's body the next morning.

Since then, Jamie had been working overtime to find out just what the hell had happened. Thanks to the prisoner from Hanes's crew, they'd been able to piece everything together. Except for what was hidden in the storage unit.

Hanes and Kader had definitely been working together overseas. Playing both sides, and playing one side off the other.

From what Jamie had said, Hanes had done all kinds of illegal shit to make himself rich, funneling the dirty money into various offshore accounts under fake company names to hide his activities. He'd planned to set Kader up to take the fall for everything, and look like a hero when he took out one of the most wanted terrorists in turn.

But Kader had figured out what was happening, and turned the tables on Hanes at the last moment. From what they could gather, he'd tracked down Sam because of her connection with Luke and her reputation as incorruptible, and sent her the letter.

The key was to a storage unit that matched the coordinates in the note. Federal agents were raiding it now. Whatever was in there would no doubt tell them the extent of Hanes's corruption. It had been enough for Hanes to kill for.

A light knock sounded on the pocket door. "Yeah," Luke said, turning to face it.

It opened to reveal Rhys and Dec standing there. "Anything on the storage unit?" Dec asked.

"Not yet." But he could guess what might be in there. And how Hanes had obtained it all.

"Sam just called," Rhys said. "The doctors might release Ben tomorrow, if he keeps improving, and if you and Nev are willing to take over his care. Sam and Ben were hoping to be able to stay with you for another week or so, until he's up to getting on a plane."

"Of course." Tomorrow was Christmas Eve. Em's favorite day of the year. She loved Christmas, but said Christmas Eve was the best because of all the anticipation built up over the course of the season. "They're welcome to stay with us as long as they want."

The hint of a smile touched Rhys's mouth. "Thanks."

Luke shook his head. "No thanks needed. You're all family." Before he could say anything else, his cell rang. He pulled it out, his pulse jumping when he saw Jamie's number. "Got news?" he asked his friend.

"Yeah."

"Hold on, I'm gonna put you on speaker. Got Dec and Rhys here with me." He hit the button and held the phone out. "Go."

"The Feds raided the storage unit a few hours ago. It was full of heroin, opium, cash and weapons. Six-million-dollars' worth."

Dec gave a low whistle and folded his arms to lean against the side of the bookcase on the far wall. Rhys's expression remained unreadable.

"Anything else?" Luke asked.

"Yeah, Kader left his laptop in there as well. Techs found enough evidence against Hanes to add over a dozen international crimes to his tally. Including blackmail, murder, and human trafficking."

Asshole. Luke made a sound of disgust. "So that's it?"

"What, you wanted more?"

Luke's mouth twisted into a half-smile. "Nope. Glad the fucker's dead." The Feds had dragged his body from the harbor the morning after the firefight at the fort.

"I am too. I wanted to update you as soon as I got the news."

"I appreciate it."

"Merry Christmas, Hutch."

"Yeah. Merry Christmas." He ended the call and looked at the others. "It's over."

It was over, yet he couldn't let it go.

Couldn't get past that this had happened here, where everyone should have been safe. Couldn't get past the thought that Em might have been the one taken if she hadn't gone into the bathroom with Nev. Or the very real threat that he might lose her yet, to an enemy he couldn't see.

When the others had gone upstairs, he entered their bedroom and locked the door. Em was still in the bath. He could smell the vanilla scent of the bath gel she used.

The bathroom door was partly open. He pushed it aside and found her in the tub, a layer of bubbles resting just below her collarbones.

She gave him a tentative smile. "Everything okay?"

"Yeah. Everything's fine." But it wasn't. And he couldn't make it fine.

A wave of protectiveness and need crashed through him. He could protect her from all kinds of threats, but not the one happening in her body right now, and that ripped him to shreds inside.

She stilled in the water, held his gaze as he strode toward the tub. "Luke?"

He was past talking, the need to claim her eclipsing everything else. He snagged a towel from the rack, then reached down and plucked her from the water.

She made a startled sound and grabbed his shoulders as he pulled her out of the tub. Wrapping the towel around her, he scooped her back up and strode out of the bathroom to their bed.

Em sat up as he placed her on the comforter, her face worried as she cupped the side of his cheek. "Luke, what's wrong?"

Everything. Everything was wrong except this.

He needed her. And he desperately craved the reassurance and oblivion only she could give him.

He plunged a hand into her hair and kissed her, absorbing her tiny jolt of surprise. He was too worked up to explain himself, his heart racing, his whole body strung taut.

But she understood. As always, Em understood without him saying anything. She cradled his head in her hands and kissed him back with equal passion, pulling him down on top of her.

Luke groaned into her mouth and reached for the bottom of his shirt, breaking the kiss only long enough to peel it over his head. He stripped everything else off, then turned back to her, pausing to drink her in.

The bathroom light was still on, spilling out the door in a trail across the floor and over their bed. Em lay on her back, totally naked, and she didn't cover herself to hide her scars.

Letting him see her fully, only a trace of uncertainty in her gaze. So fucking beautiful and brave it made his heart clench.

He stretched out on top of her, giving her his weight and warmth, then stroked her hair back from her forehead and bent to fuse their mouths together. She welcomed him with a soft hum and wound her limbs around him, drawing him closer.

He rocked into her, the rigid length of his cock cradled against her softness. Wanting inside her. But not until she was as hungry for him as he was for her.

He kissed his way down her neck, his hands moving lower, paving the way for the path of his lips until they caressed the scar she hated so much on the right side of her chest.

Her muscles tensed a little but he kissed every inch of her scar while his fingers played with her taut nipple. She gasped, lifting into his touch, asking for more.

He rewarded her by taking the point into his mouth, sucking while his fingers caressed her velvety skin, following the line of her ribs to her abdomen, then down to feather along the inside of her thighs.

She held her head to him and parted her legs, her breathing speeding up. He released her nipple to nuzzle the slight curve of her belly, trailing his fingertips up to the soft folds between her legs. She moaned when he touched her there, but he would make her even wetter.

He needed his mouth on her. His tongue on her and inside her.

His hands curled around her hips, holding her still

while he settled his mouth over her. Em gave a soft, keening cry and gripped his hair. He held her steady, keeping her in place while he stroked and caressed.

Gentle and slow, doing all the things he knew she loved. When her breathing turned erratic and her thighs started trembling, he shifted lower and eased his tongue into her.

"Luke," she breathed, her hips lifting, eyes closed, her face awash in pleasure.

He loved seeing her like this. Got off on the sensual tension thrumming through her body, and knowing he was making her feel good.

With one last decadent caress over her clit, he eased back and turned her onto her knees. He was hard and throbbing, the need to bury himself inside her tearing through him.

Guiding her upper body down to the bedding with a hand on her upper back, he gripped her hips and settled the head of his cock against her core. She shifted restlessly, her cheek on the comforter as she angled her head to watch him with heavy-lidded eyes.

Luke leaned over her, kissed her shoulder, her cheek, the edge of her lips while he reached beneath her to cup her mound. Instantly she grabbed his hand and began rubbing her clit against his fingers, holding him right where she needed him.

"Need you," he said in a rough voice.

She nodded, rocking her hips in a sexy rhythm. "Need you too."

He leaned over to open the drawer of her nightstand and pulled out her favorite toy. Positioning it between her legs, he turned it on low and moved it over her clit, knowing he had the right spot when she gasped.

He tightened his free hand on her hip, turned up the speed and eased forward, seating himself with a slow, deep thrust that made them both moan.

Luke paused, shuddering as her warmth closed around him. She whimpered and kept moving, each tiny motion of her hips massaging his cock.

There were no words now, only the gentle hum of the toy and the sound of their bodies as they moved together. He fine-tuned the placement of the toy, finding just the right spot on her clit.

Em moaned, the look on her face and the way she clenched around him telling him she was close. He kept his thrusts smooth and steady, even as he wanted to plunge deep and hard. His restraint was rewarded by her erotic whimpers while he stroked in and out of her slick heat.

Pleasure drenched him, dragging him closer and closer to the edge. She went over with a muffled sob. Luke wrapped his arm around her waist, holding her close, savoring the way she writhed through her release.

Finally, she reached down to turn off the toy. He set it aside, breathing fast, the need to come making him shake.

But he needed more. Needed to be face to face with her.

Easing out of her warmth, he rolled her to her back. Em smiled drowsily up at him and drew him close, reaching down to close her fingers around his rigid length. He closed his eyes and shuddered, shifting closer.

Em guided him into her, wrapped her arms and legs around him. Holding her gaze, he thrust deep, a low growl coming from him.

He squeezed his eyes shut and pressed closer, burying his face in her hair. Her silken arms gathered him closer. Enveloping him with her warmth and love.

Luke slid both arms around her, clutching her to him. Wanting closer. To stay locked in her forever.

"Em," he choked out, driving faster. Nearing the edge of oblivion and never wanting it to end.

Em murmured something and kissed the side of his face, holding him tight. "Let go," she whispered. "I've got you."

His arms tightened around her as the pleasure crested. Release punched through him, along with a savage sense of possessiveness and satisfaction. She was his, and nothing or no one was taking her from him.

Breathing hard, heart racing, Luke groaned and sagged into her embrace. She held him, those soft, magical hands running slowly up and down his damp back. Stroking his hair, his shoulders.

He couldn't let go. Couldn't bear to tear himself away from her.

"Love you, Luke," she murmured drowsily.

He kissed the side of her neck and held her tight. "Love you too."

Holding her in the darkness, he wished he could freeze time. Because they were supposed to get a call about the test results tomorrow.

And he'd never been more afraid of anything in his life.

Chapter Seventeen

Emily bustled around the kitchen the next morning, humming along to the old-fashioned Christmas carols playing softly in the background. She'd slept in until seven and woken rested and refreshed in Luke's arms.

That was one of her favorite things about having him back. Waking up with him wrapped around her, just lying there in the quiet listening to his even breathing and soaking up the warmth and sense of safety at being close to him.

Last night had been intense, him desperate to connect and her desperate to soothe him. Because of the call that could come at any moment.

She swept the thought aside, refusing to get stuck on it. It was Christmas Eve, her favorite day of the year, and they all had so much to be grateful for.

Sam and Ben were still at the hospital, but Ben's fever was gone and his vitals were strong. If he kept improving the way he had, he was supposed to be discharged late in the afternoon—as long as he did as she and Nev told him. Otherwise he'd find himself back in the hospital in short order.

While on lockdown at the rental safehouse with the others she'd lost the better part of two days in her holiday preparations. She had to make up for lost time and wanted everything ready by the time Sam and Ben got here. Even if he might not have much of an appetite to begin with, she planned to have all kinds of things to tempt him with, just in case.

"Holy, how much butter did you guys buy?"

She looked up as Christa and Bryn entered the kitchen, then glanced at the countertop beside her. They were right. There was a lot of butter. "I dunno. A lot."

"I'll say," Christa said, laughing as she took in all the blocks Emily had set out to soften on the island. "What are you making?"

"Looks like she's making a little of everything," Bryn remarked, staring at it all.

"What can we help with?" Christa asked, already pushing up the sleeves of her sweater.

"Pie filling or cookie dough would be great." Emily pushed a lock of hair back from her forehead with the back of one flour-covered hand and resumed rolling the pastry for the pies. She had three different kinds going: apple, pecan and pumpkin, and three different kinds of homemade cookies as well.

She passed Christa a package of pecans to chop, and Bryn a bowl of shortbread dough. "I asked Ben's mother what his favorite Christmas treats were so I could have some ready when he gets here," she said. "So, an apple pie for Ben, coming up. And when they arrive, Sam can take a break and let the rest of us take over the nursing duties."

"Aww." Christa stepped up to put an arm around her shoulders and hugged her. "This is why everyone loves you, Em. You and your big, squishy heart."

That made her smile. "I do have a squishy heart." It had caused her a lot of pain over the years, but she

156

wouldn't have changed it for anything.

Even her situation with Luke she wouldn't have changed. As devastating as it had been for him to walk out on her and Rayne all those years ago, it made having him now a thousand times sweeter. "Where's Nev?"

"Right here." She walked in looking sleepy but content, her hair loose around her shoulders. "Had a late night last night at the hospital. Let's just say we're gonna have our hands full making Ben stay in bed. When I left, he was trying to walk himself to the bathroom, after having pulled out his catheter."

"Well, if he doesn't behave, we'll put it back in for him," Emily said, making the others laugh. But she was serious. Squishy heart or no, she was a firm nurse. Ben wasn't getting away with anything here that he wouldn't on her ward.

The murmur of voices reached her from the back porch, then the French door opened. Luke strode through with Rayne, Dec and Rhys.

Luke caught her gaze and gave her a slow smile that set her pulse pounding. Last night had been so damn good. She'd only ever been able to let go like that with him, maybe because he made her feel safe even on a subconscious level.

"You didn't waste any time," he remarked, sauntering over to her.

"You know me. Gotta keep busy."

He hummed in agreement and wrapped his arms around her from behind, his lips on the side of her neck. "Need a nap?"

It was ten in the morning. "No," she said on a laugh, knowing sleeping was the last thing on his mind. "But you can help me decorate the cookies." She looked around at the others. "Do you mind?"

She got uncertain looks from Dec and Rhys, but in the end, everyone pitched in. It was adorable to see a huge, hard man like Rhys piping royal icing onto the gingerbread people, and Dec adding chocolate candies for the eyes and buttons. Bryn took a break in chopping the pecans to take lots of pictures of them.

Luke rolled out the sugar cookie dough, then cut them with her great-grandmother's cutters while Christa and Nev worked on the shortbreads. "I can feel my pancreas giving out already," he said, eyeing all the treats being made, and Emily chuckled.

After finishing the icing outline around the edge of one gingerbread cookie, Rhys paused, frowning as he looked at the spices set out on the counter. "What's this?"

Emily glanced up and smiled. "Your brother." She'd put them on the counter because they reminded her of him and made her smile.

Rhys smirked and went back to his piping. "Figures." A ring tone went off. He set down the bag of icing and pulled out his phone, then answered. "Hey, what's up?" He paused, straightening. "Really? Yeah, absolutely. I'll be there in fifteen."

"What?" Emily asked as he ended the call. Everyone was watching him.

"Ben's being discharged now."

"Now?" She narrowed her eyes in suspicion, wondering how he'd managed to get them to release him hours ahead of schedule. "I won't ask how or why."

"Probably for the best," he answered, one side of his mouth tugging upward. He wiped his hands on a kitchen towel. "I'd better get going."

"We'd better get going too," she said to the others, untying her apron. "Christa, can you throw the shortbreads and sugar cookies into the wall oven? It's already preheated. Start watching them at eleven minutes." She gestured to Luke. "Help me get the bed ready."

She hurried upstairs to get fresh linens. They'd decided to put a bed in Luke's study for Ben, so he wouldn't have to worry about stairs until he was stronger. And there was a shower in the downstairs bathroom two doors down.

Emily grabbed clean sheets, a spare comforter and a new pillow, and carried them downstairs. Luke brought in the foldable frame and foam mattress from the garage and brought them into his study.

Just as they were finishing dressing the bed together, her cell phone rang on Luke's desk. He grabbed it and seemed to freeze for an instant before his gaze shot to hers. Just as quickly he looked away and answered it. "Luke Hutchinson."

Emily's heart started to pound. Oh, lord. Was it...

He turned away from her as he listened, and dread tightened her insides like a fist. The oncologist. Had to be. Calling to give them the results of the tests.

She straightened, stood there staring at Luke's broad back while the tension drew tighter and tighter in her gut. All the fear she'd buried these last few days and managed to forget about due to everything that had happened came rushing back in a terrifying wave.

"Yeah, she's right here." He turned to face her, the same dread she was feeling reflected in his face.

And that frightened her more. Luke didn't get scared. And he never let it show. Oh shit, no...

"It's the oncologist," he said, watching her. "He has the results."

She swallowed, suddenly cold and feeling shaky as hell. But she squared her shoulders and lifted her chin. She'd fought this battle before and won, at least temporarily. She would fight it again.

"Put him on speaker so we can both hear." She wanted him to hear it firsthand, so she wouldn't have to repeat anything. Luke did.

"Hi, Mark," she said, every muscle in her body tight.

"Emily, hi."

"Hi," she said, her voice barely more than a whisper. She wanted to be brave, especially in front of Luke, but inside she was terrified. When he stepped over to wrap a steadying arm around her shoulders, she leaned into him gratefully. Okay. She was ready. Whatever the doctor was about to say, they would face it together. "You have the test results?"

"Yes." He paused.

Emily shut her eyes, bracing herself.

"Merry Christmas, Emily. You're cancer free."

Her eyes sprang open, unsure she'd heard him correctly. She stared at the phone, aware of Luke going completely rigid next to her, the words slowly penetrating the haze in her frantic mind. "Wh-what?" she whispered, hardly daring to believe what he'd just said.

"The tests came back negative. All of them. You're cancer free."

Her hand flew to her mouth as a sob burst free. She turned toward Luke, reaching for him. He set the phone on his desk and grabbed her, hauling her against him so tightly he lifted her off the floor.

"Oh my God," she choked out. "Oh my God..."

"Em," he whispered hoarsely, crushing her to him.

Dizzy with relief, she lifted her head to look up into his face. His eyes were filled with tears, his love for her shining through them. "I'm okay," she said, incredulous. Ecstatic.

Luke's face broke into a smile and he laughed through his tears. "Yeah, you are."

She laughed too and then clung to him again, letting her tears slip free, even as his wet the side of her neck. *I'm okay...*

The pocket door slid open. They both turned to find Rayne standing there, his face a mask of concern, and the others all gathered behind him. Christa, Nev. Bryn and Dec.

"What happened?" Rayne demanded as Christa stepped up beside him, watching her worriedly. "What did the doctor say?"

Emily sniffed and wiped the heel of one hand across her eyes, smiling at their son. "He said I'm cancer free."

Rayne's eyes widened a fraction. He glanced at Luke, as though checking to make sure it was true. When Luke nodded, Rayne sagged, his eyes closing as everyone else erupted into a cheer.

Rayne collected himself, then came over and gathered her into a fierce hug that made the back of her throat ache with a rush of fresh tears. "Thank God. I love you, Mom."

"Love you too," she whispered back. Christa was beaming as she came toward them, her own eyes wet. "And you," Emily said, lifting an arm to include her daughter-in-law in the embrace. Over Christa's shoulder she grinned at the others. "And the rest of you too. Get in here, y'all."

The next thing she knew, she was engulfed from all sides in a group hug. She laughed and soaked it all up, dizzy with relief.

Through her laughter came the peal of the doorbell. "They're here," she said excitedly. The knot dispersed, freeing her from the center, and everyone flowed out of the study and down the hall to the foyer.

Emily opened the door and smiled at Ben. He looked pale and tired, ready to keel over at any moment, but he wore a slight grin as he stood there, bent over slightly, Rhys on one side of him and Sam on the other. "Hi," he said weakly. "Merry Christmas."

"Merry Christmas, Ben," she answered, and carefully enfolded him in a hug before stepping back to help him inside.

While everyone else greeted him, Emily bustled around readying everything to make him as comfortable as possible. She had never been so happy as she escorted him to his temporary bedroom, her heart full to bursting.

Take that, cancer, she told the whisper in her head, now silent.

This was already far and away the best Christmas she'd ever had.

—The End—

Dear reader,

Thank you for reading *Silent Night, Deadly Night*. If you'd like to stay in touch with me and be the first to learn about new releases you can:

- Join my newsletter at: http://kayleacross.com/v2/newsletter/

- Find me on Facebook: https://www.facebook.com/KayleaCrossAuthor/

- Follow me on Twitter: https://twitter.com/kayleacross

- Follow me on Instagram: https://www.instagram.com/kaylea_cross_author

Also, please consider leaving a review at your favorite online book retailer. It helps other readers discover new books.

Happy reading,
Kaylea

Excerpt from **Lethal Protector**
Rifle Creek Series #3
By Kaylea Cross
Copyright © 2021 Kaylea Cross

Prologue

"Is this seat taken?"

At the sound of that deep voice beside her, Tala looked up from her lunch at the base mess hall table and gasped. "Brax!"

She jumped out of her chair, a huge smile spreading across her face, and barely resisted the urge to throw her arms around him. That kind of fraternization while in uniform was a definite no-no. "What are you doing here in Kandahar?" The latest rumors she'd heard had said his unit was up north somewhere.

His sexy grin made her heart somersault. His honey-toned skin was even darker with his tan, and his full, dark beard made him even more ruggedly masculine. "Just got in early this morning. Heard from Tate that you were here, so I thought I'd track you down and say hi."

Her brother, who was friends with him and Braxton's best buddy Mason. "I'm glad you did. You're looking good." Even more gorgeous than she remembered, and she thought about him a lot more than she should.

"Thanks," he murmured, looking uncomfortable at her compliment. He gestured to the chair beside her. "May I?"

"Yes, of course." She sat back down, put an elbow on the table and propped her chin in her hand to admire him, touched that he'd taken the trouble to come find her. "How long are you here for?"

"Couple days, maybe, just depends."

On whether they get actionable intel on their next target. "Is Mason with you?" They were both JTF2 operators, members of Canada's most elite counterterrorism unit. Hence the beard, due to relaxed grooming regulations in the SOF units.

"He's around. Not working with him directly much right now, though."

Because Brax was a sniper. He worked with a small team mostly, sometimes only him and whoever was acting as his spotter. "Ah. Well, tell him I said hi when you see him."

"I will." He leaned back in his chair a bit, giving her a slow smile that heated her insides. And she was almost positive he had no clue he had that effect on her. "Everything good with you?"

"Yeah. I've only got another five weeks before I rotate home. I can't wait to see Rylee." Her teenage daughter back in Kelowna. "We video chat a lot, but it's not the same." Seeing Braxton made her feel homesick, reminding her of all she'd left behind.

"No. She staying with your parents?"

"Yeah, they're taking good care of her. They even moved into our place so she could stay in her own surroundings while I'm over here." Her parents were awesome, had always been there for her, including supporting her as a single teenage mom trying to learn how to take care of a baby.

He nodded, opened his mouth to say something else, stopped, and pulled his phone out of his pocket. He gave the screen a cursory glance, then tucked it away with a sigh. "Really sorry, but I gotta go." He stood.

"I do too." She wished they'd had more time together. But duty called. "Hey, if you end up being here for a few more days and have some time to kill, drop me a text and we'll meet up for a coffee or whatever. If you want," she rushed to add.

"I'd like that." His deep brown eyes were warm as he gazed down at her, the corners crinkling slightly with the hint of a smile. He was fond of her, but she wasn't sure if there was anything more for him than that. She wished there was. "Take care of yourself."

"Yeah, you too." She allowed herself to watch him walk away for a few seconds before forcing her attention back to her half-eaten meal. Except her appetite was now gone. Seeing Braxton reminded her too much of home—and also what she could never have.

Him. Braxton was married to his unit, and tended not to let anyone in. There was no place in his life for anything else, including her. But somehow that still wasn't enough to make her stop dreaming of him or imagining them together.

Returning her tray to the stack by the door, she left the mess hall and hurried back across base toward her barracks, anxious to get this next patrol over with so she could enjoy some downtime tomorrow. Rylee had exams this week and would no doubt be up late cramming. Maybe they could have a quick video call tomorrow.

Seated in the back of the APV fifteen minutes later, she found her concentration fragmented as they headed outside the wire and out of the relative protection of the base. Their mission today was to provide security for some brass on the way out to some rural villages to foster relations with the local farmers in the region.

Communication buzzed back and forth between the officers in charge up ahead of them in the convoy, and the sergeant riding shotgun in her vehicle. She stared out the small armored window at the dun-colored landscape, her mind wandering back to Braxton. He'd gone to the trouble of seeking her out today. Did that mean anything? She wanted it to.

Twenty-plus miles into their trip, the vehicles slowed as they approached a large village. EOD teams had been busy here during the night, clearing the road of any mines or IEDs in preparation for their arrival today. Still, Tala tensed, her pulse speeding up as she tightened her grip on her C7 rifle.

She jerked when bullets raked the side of their vehicle, sucking in a sharp breath as her heart rate shot up.

"Contact right, two hundred meters," her sergeant barked into the radio.

Tala glanced around, looking for signs of the enemy. More rounds pinged off the armored plating and kicked up puffs of gray-brown dust as they hit the ground.

The sergeant twisted around in his seat to say something, face tense, but a fireball exploded at the front of the convoy. The force of it shook their vehicle.

The radio traffic surged as the two vehicles in front of them opened, the soldiers pouring out to assume a defensive position. Tala forced back her fear and exited her vehicle with the others, rifle to her shoulder as she searched for a target. She flinched and ducked when another explosion rocked the air, another vehicle ahead of them going up in flames.

Her sergeant was yelling at them over the noise, ordering them away from the vehicle. Tala reacted immediately, glancing around for the nearest cover. She was in a bad spot, out in the open, midway between the road and the irrigation ditch to the left.

Tala ran for it.

She only made it a few steps before a blast of heat seared her back. The air rushed from her lungs as the force of the nearby explosion shot her forward, lifting her off the ground.

She landed hard on her side and scrambled upright, her ears ringing, and did a quick assessment. The APV she'd just been standing next to was a burning mass of metal. Two people were lying on the ground.

People all around her were running for cover. She had to help the wounded.

You're not hit. Get up.

Shaken, she rolled to her feet and rushed for the closest casualty.

Brilliant white light seared her retinas a second later. More heat, this time beneath and in front of her. Then she was airborne.

The world turned upside down. She hit the ground hard on her back and lay there staring up at the smoke-filled sky. It took a moment for her brain to kick back online, the world spinning around her, the stench of cordite stinging her nostrils and her mouth filled with dust and blood. Shit. Had she been hit?

Get up. Get up.

But she couldn't. Could only push up on her elbows, her mind reeling, her body refusing to obey. She was hurt.

Rylee.

Her daughter's face flashed in her mind, galvanizing her. *Have to get behind cover.*

Through the thick cloud of dust, a figure appeared above her. A man. Kneeling down beside her. "Tala."

She blinked up at him, stunned but recognizing that voice. *Braxton.* Where had he come from?

She tried to respond but only a wheeze came out. Something was wrong.

He was reaching down, past the limited field of her blurry vision toward her legs. She felt tight pressure around her right calf. "Medic!" he shouted over his shoulder. "I need a medic over here!"

Tala went rigid, her heart shooting into her throat as her gaze snapped to his broad back, blocking her view. Was she injured? She didn't feel anything except the stinging from where the blast wave had hit her in the face and hands.

She struggled to lift her head, tried to see what had happened to her, but Braxton was in the way. Two more people ran up to help.

And then Braxton spun around to straddle her torso, leaning down to cup her face in his hands. He stared down at her, face grim, his dark eyes holding her immobile. "You're gonna be okay. Just keep looking at me."

He was trying to prevent her from seeing her lower body.

Fear tore through her. Gunfire rattled all around them, the stench of burning metal stinging her nostrils. She struggled to turn her head to see past him, see what the other two people were doing to her.

And then the pain hit. Vicious and hot. Searing through her right calf.

She sucked in a ragged breath, eyes squeezing shut as a cry of agony came out. She instinctively thrashed, trying to escape it. *My leg...*

Strong hands held her in place. Braxton had his hands clamped on her shoulders, pinning her down, his weight anchoring her hips. His urgent voice sounded in her ears but she couldn't understand him, couldn't focus through the pain and terror.

Oh God, oh God, oh God... She was shaking now. Freezing cold in spite of the heat, her stomach roiling.

"Don't move, Tal. Just stay still. You're gonna be okay."

Tala forced her eyes open, shock taking hold. Was he lying? She was hyperventilating, the fear and pain colliding. She met his gaze for a second, then slid hers to the left.

Through the dust and smoke, she saw a boot lying in the dust a few meters away. Several inches of bloody bone and tissue were sticking out of it.

She stared at it in horror, reality hitting her like a

sledgehammer.

Oh my God, that's my foot.

Gagging, she rolled her head to the side to retch into the blood-spattered dirt.

End Excerpt

ABOUT THE AUTHOR

NY Times and USA Today Bestselling author Kaylea Cross writes edge-of-your-seat military romantic suspense. Her work has won many awards, including the Daphne du Maurier Award of Excellence, and has been nominated multiple times for the National Readers' Choice Awards. A Registered Massage Therapist by trade, Kaylea is also an avid gardener, artist, Civil War buff, Special Ops aficionado, belly dance enthusiast and former nationally-carded softball pitcher. She lives in Vancouver, BC with her husband and family.

You can visit Kaylea at www.kayleacross.com. If you would like to be notified of future releases, please join her newsletter.

http://kayleacross.com/v2/newsletter/

Complete Booklist

ROMANTIC SUSPENSE

Kill Devil Hills Series
Undercurrent
Submerged
Adrift

Rifle Creek Series
Lethal Edge
Lethal Temptation
Lethal Protector

Vengeance Series
Stealing Vengeance
Covert Vengeance
Explosive Vengeance
Toxic Vengeance
Beautiful Vengeance

Crimson Point Series
Fractured Honor
Buried Lies
Shattered Vows
Rocky Ground
Broken Bonds

DEA FAST Series
Falling Fast
Fast Kill
Stand Fast
Strike Fast
Fast Fury
Fast Justice
Fast Vengeance

Colebrook Siblings Trilogy
Brody's Vow
Wyatt's Stand
Easton's Claim

Hostage Rescue Team Series
Marked
Targeted
Hunted
Disavowed
Avenged
Exposed
Seized
Wanted
Betrayed
Reclaimed
Shattered
Guarded

Titanium Security Series
Ignited
Singed
Burned
Extinguished
Rekindled
Blindsided: A Titanium Christmas novella

Bagram Special Ops Series
Deadly Descent
Tactical Strike
Lethal Pursuit
Danger Close
Collateral Damage
Never Surrender (a MacKenzie Family novella)

Suspense Series
Out of Her League
Cover of Darkness
No Turning Back
Relentless
Absolution
Silent Night, Deadly Night

PARANORMAL ROMANCE
Empowered Series
Darkest Caress

HISTALACAL ROMANCE
The Vacant Chair

EROTIC ROMANCE (writing as *Callie Croix*)
Deacon's Touch
Dillon's Claim
No Holds Barred
Touch Me
Let Me In
Covert Seduction

CPSIA information can be obtained
at www.ICGtesting.com
Printed in the USA
LVHW041919220721
693425LV00008B/1222